BIG

Love

K.M. SCOTT

2020 Copper Key Media, LLC
Copyright © 2020 Copper Key Media, LLC
Print Edition

Published in the United States

ISBN-13: 978-1-7346645-4-6

Cover Design: Sweet 'N Spicy Designs

Books by K.M. Scott

Crash Into Me (Heart of Stone #1)
Fall Into Me (Heart of Stone #2)
Give In To Me (Heart of Stone #3)
Heart of Stone Volume One
Ever After (Heart of Stone #4)
A Heart of Stone Christmas (Heart of Stone #5)
Return To Me (Heart of Stone #6)
Forever With Me (Heart of Stone #7)
Heart of Stone Volume Two
Hard As Stone (Heart of Stone #8)
Set In Stone (Heart of Stone #9)
Silent As A Stone (Heart of Stone #10)
Heart of Stone Volume Three
All of Me (Heart of Stone #11)

Temptation (Club X #1)
Surrender (Club X #2)
Possession (Club X #3)
Satisfaction (Club X #4)
Acceptance (Club X #5)
The Complete Club X Series

If I Dream (Corrupted Love #1)
If You Fight (Corrupted Love #2)
If We Fall (Corrupted Love #3)

Crave (Addicted To You #1)
Adore (Addicted To You #2)
Shatter (Addicted To You #3)
Claim (Addicted To You #4)
The Addicted To You Series

In The Darkness (Project Artemis #1)
After The Storm (Project Artemis #2)
Behind The Scenes (Project Artemis #3)

Hard Work (Finding The One #1)
Big Love (Finding The One #2)

Books by K.M. Scott writing as Gabrielle Bisset

Blood Avenged (Sons of Navarus #1)
Blood Betrayed (Sons of Navarus #2)
Blood Spirit (Sons of Navarus #3)
Blood Prophecy (Sons of Navarus #4)
Blood Craving (Sons of Navarus #5)
Blood Eclipse (Sons of Navarus #6)
Blood Ascendant (Sons of Navarus #7)

Stolen Destiny (Destined Ones Duology #1)
Destiny Redeemed (Destined Ones Duology #2)

Love's Master
Masquerade
The Victorian Erotic Romance Trilogy

To Lindsey Buckingham for the title inspiration and to every funny guy who got me to get naked because of his sense of humor.

BIG LOVE

Clare Schiffer has always lived in the small town of Hansonville, but she dreams of more than the ordinary life that seems so acceptable to everyone she knows. Especially when it comes to love.

She's had mediocre love in the past. Now if she's going to fall in love, it needs to be big and unforgettable.

And just as she begins to believe that only exists in movies, a brand new man comes to town. Matt is good looking and charming, and in no time at all, he's won over everyone in Hansonville.

Except for Clare. Matt isn't sure of much in life, but he knows one thing for certain. He's going to make the beautiful brunette with the standoffish way his, and when he does, the past won't matter for either of them.

CHAPTER ONE

Clare

HANSONVILLE HADN'T SEEN this much excitement since that one time last summer a circus tour bus broke down out on Highway 27. No less than twenty-six clowns in full makeup complete with red noses and curly wigs, a burly sword swallower with the hairiest chest anyone had ever seen, and a man who was supposedly the world's tallest man walked single-file all the way into town to the Patriot Restaurant to order lunch as they waited for new transportation to come for them.

Traffic came to a halt on Main Street, backing up cars all the way to the statue of George Washington standing proudly at the entrance to town. Once citizens realized who they were, practically all work stopped so everyone could scurry over to the restaurant to gawk at nearly thirty clowns and their friends eating grilled cheese and bologna sandwiches, the signature lunch at the Patriot.

Today's excitement seemed less interesting as there were no clowns or hairy sword swallowers. Still, finding a man out on the side of the highway who had no memory whatsoever of how he got there or who he was certainly ranked as a unique occurrence for Hansonville.

"Did you hear about him?" the short woman with beady eyes from the coffee shop said in a hushed voice to no one in particular in the crowd standing outside the ER doors at Penn Valley Hospital. "I heard he couldn't even tell them his name."

"I heard they didn't find a car or anything. Just him lying on the side of the road in the weeds," the round-bellied man who ran over from pumping gas at the station nearby said to her in response.

A thin woman who looked to be in her early twenties added with a giggle, "I heard someone say they thought he might be a gigolo."

A gigolo in Hansonville. I couldn't stop myself from rolling my eyes. Ridiculous. Why anyone would think a gigolo would even drive through our sleepy little town made me wonder if everyone around me had lost their minds.

Such was my small town when something out of the ordinary happened. Rumors spread like wildfire, even though the policeman who escorted the ambulance to the hospital had been overheard giving the actual details of the unfortunate stranger's story to a nurse who met him at the doors not two minutes before.

But why bother with the truth since fiction and wild rumors are so much more interesting?

I stepped back out of the way and craned my neck to see what the mystery man looked like as they wheeled him into the Penn Valley Hospital on a gurney. Not that seeing someone as they lay flat on their back being whisked past you was much to go on, but he had dark hair and a strong face.

At least that's what I thought in the second I saw him. He seemed tall—well, not circus performer tallest man in the world tall—but from what I could see, I was sticking with the description of him being tall.

The crowd began to break up as the doors closed behind the gurney, but since I was at the hospital to visit my friend Emma, I followed the stranger and his official entourage inside. I found the crowd outside had been small in comparison to the group that had formed in the hallway leading to the ER. Noisy from people voicing their opinions on the situation, it felt more like a convention than a hospital.

Emma waved at me from the nurses' station at the center of the floor and yelled, "Clare, down here!" Dressed in bright pink scrubs, she stood out in the sea of spectators filling the hallway.

Weaving through the onlookers, some of whom worked at the hospital and others who had snuck in uninvited, I made my way toward her. Finally, I reached her after pushing my way through the last few busybodies dying to learn anything about the stranger found out on Highway 27.

"Can you believe this? It's been like this ever since word came in about the guy. I can barely hear myself think," she said in exasperation, her hands flailing as she spoke and her dark eyes wide in frustration at what had become of her workplace.

Emma was the consummate professional. She loved to be fun and spontaneous outside of work, but when it came to her job, she liked order and as little excitement as possible so she could help her patients. Definitely not what surrounded her at the moment.

"What are you doing down here in the ER? You're usually two floors up."

She looked around at all the people and shook her head. "It's all hands-on deck today, so they moved all of us around to make sure the ER was staffed to handle all this nonsense. Security already cleared out one bunch who got here right after the story broke. I assume they'll get this group out soon too."

Raising her voice, she added, "At least I hope so."

All this uproar made my friend uneasy. She'd become a nurse to help people, not to practice crowd control.

She wasn't wrong either.

The place was a madhouse. It was totally inappropriate behavior for grown adults to be displaying, and in a hospital no less. Penn Valley Hospital had a reputation as a sleepy kind of place on most days, and that's the way she liked her work to be. Throngs of people hanging out in the ER hallway made her edgy, and I suspected at any moment she would blow up and order every single one of them to vacate the premises.

"You know how this town is, Emma," I yelled over the voices around us chattering about the mystery man and who he could be. "We don't have a lot happening here, so things like this or that bus of stranded clowns last summer get everyone excited. It's silly, but it's not surprising."

She rolled her eyes and tugged my arm to lead me to a quieter place. "I'd rather the clowns. At least they went to the Patriot," she said, huffing in disgust as she pushed me into a break room at the end of the hall.

I laughed at her attitude. Other than me, Emma was one of the few people in town who wasn't old but didn't mind how slow and quiet Hansonville was. Well, at least when it came to her work.

But to me, our little town was at its best when it was boring old Hansonville. While everyone else wished for more exciting things to happen, I was content to live in small-town America.

At least for the most part.

"You and I are probably the only two people around who don't care about Mr. Mystery Man, you know that?" I joked as I sat down at a small table in the break room with her.

Rubbing her temples, she nodded. "Unless he's my knight in shining armor come to sweep me off my feet and onto his white horse, I don't give one damn about him. All that I know is he comes with an awful lot of noisy people interrupting my work."

"I don't think he's got a white horse. In fact, if what I heard is true, he didn't even have a car when they found him out on the highway. He was just lying in the grass on the side of the road."

Emma scowled. "I heard. So no knight in shining armor. Just some drifter guy who probably had too much to drink and lost his way."

"Probably."

She waved her hand and dismissed the whole thing going on outside the break room door.

"Enough of that. Are we still on for tapas tonight?"

"You know, those aren't really tapas, Emma. I know the Patriot tries, but a few plates of bar food aren't really what I'd call tapas."

Shrugging, she shook her head. "I don't care if all they do is put some corn chips in a bowl. It's better than what I have in my fridge at the moment, and it's a chance for us to have a few drinks and relax after a hard day at work. From what I've seen this afternoon, I'm going to need at least a few. So, what do you say? Can you tear yourself away from watching TV tonight and try to have a good time?"

"Always giving me a hard time about that. There's nothing wrong with a single girl filling her time with TV."

Emma scrunched her face up like she'd just sucked on a lemon. "I think that means something entirely different from what you mean. I can't discuss the idea of what you do every night right now, though, since I have to head out to that mob in about twenty seconds. So are we on or not?"

I really didn't want to come into town just a few hours after going home, but looking across the table as she gave me the puppy dog eyes look, I didn't have the heart to say no. "Fine. Phony tapas it is instead of Clare's Midweek Sitcom

Fest."

Standing from the table, she chuckled. "Seriously, you need to rename what you do alone at nights. People are going to think you're some sad old maid. Who watches TV like that anymore?"

As I followed her out into the madness again, I said, "I don't go around telling people that I stay at home and watch old TV shows. That sounds weird. I only tell you."

She looked back at me and smiled. "Well, I still think you need to change up your nightly routine. Or even better, maybe you could say yes to one of the guys at the Patriot so you don't have to watch old reruns of the Andy Griffith Show every night. Ever think of that?"

"To be honest, no. I'm not interested in spending my nights with Hansonville guys. They don't have what I want."

"And that is?" she called back at me.

"I want what can't be found in this town. I want big love, not some mediocre, run-of-the-mill relationship. So my answer will continue to be no to all those guys at the Patriot."

Emma rolled her eyes at my lofty romantic ideals. "Whatever. I'll see you at eight. Look for me at the back booth critiquing the egg rolls and cheese dip."

We pushed through the crowd and stopped in

front of the area where the stranger sat in a bed. Cleaned up, his face showed cuts from the bushes he'd probably fallen into on the side of the road. Still, he was definitely attractive, even more so now that he was alert.

"He definitely isn't from around here," she said as we stared at the man as the doctor lifted his shirt to examine him, showing a great set of pecs and washboard abs that had clearly seen time in a gym and quite recently.

Definitely not. The guys in town never looked that buff.

I tore my gaze away from his muscular body and smiled at Emma. "Still think he's just some drunk drifter?"

She pursed her lips and grinned. "Probably not. Maybe I need to find out about this guy. He might have knight in shining armor in him yet."

"I'll leave you to the knight. See you at eight, and don't be late or I'll eat all the tapas on you."

My threat made her finally look away from the hot mystery man. "Don't you dare. But if they're olives, feel free. Those were disgusting last time."

"Deal. See you then!"

I LEFT HER gawking at the newest guy in town and headed down a few blocks to the Hansonville Veterinary Clinic where I worked as a vet tech.

The parking lot had only my car and the vet's, probably because everyone in town was more interested in the human sitting in the Penn Valley ER than their pets.

Laney, another of the techs who worked there, sat behind the desk playing on the computer and popped her head up when I came through the front door. A few years out of high school, she still looked like a teenager with her big blue eyes and round face made even rounder looking because she wore a ponytail all the time.

"Would you be okay taking over, Clare? I thought I'd go out for lunch today," she said with a guilty smile.

I knew what she was doing. Laney never left the office for lunch or any other reason. She brought a carefully packed lunch with a sandwich, soup, and a salad every day in an insulated carrier so nothing spoiled on the three-block walk from her house to the vet's every morning before she could put it in the refrigerator.

But the lure of the strange man from Highway 27 beckoned, obviously.

Leaning over her desk, I saw she had been reading what the Hansonville Times posted online about the man. "Lunch, huh?"

"Well, it's not every day that we get this kind of excitement in town, you know. I just want to check it out."

I held my hands up in surrender and smiled. "No judgment here. I was just at the hospital and I can safely say you're not the only person in town who's curious about the mystery man."

Her big eyes grew even wider. "Does anyone know his name yet?"

"I don't think so," I said, shaking my head. "I heard he has amnesia. He doesn't seem to know who he is or how he got out there on the side of the road."

"Ooooh, I love a mystery!" she cooed as she grabbed her purse and came out from behind the desk.

"I bet your husband does too, Laney," I joked, taking the chance to tease her since she routinely liked to comment about my still being single at twenty-eight.

Her smile slid from her face and she huffed her answer out. "It's not like that. I love Mark. He knows that. It's just that when someone new comes to town, I like to find out about them. There's nothing wrong with that."

I squeezed her arm and nodded. "Again, no judgment here. Take your time. Last I saw, he was in the ER, but the crowd was pretty big, so you might have to fight your way in if you want to get a good look at him."

My warning seemed to put a damper on her excitement and she sighed. "Maybe I'll just grab a sandwich at the Patriot and see what I can find out there. I wouldn't want to have to fight anyone just to get the news."

Taking a seat behind the desk, I said, "Good idea. I'll be here, so no problem. Enjoy your lunch."

She'd be leaving for college soon and I found myself thinking that I'd miss the sweet girl who had, admittedly, ended up making my job much easier. She'd been quiet and kind, and that's all I required from a coworker really.

Laney reminded me about the doctor's early afternoon appointments and hurried out the door to go find out about this new person in town. Not that she wanted to do it for any reason other than simple curiosity. It certainly couldn't be because the newspaper had described the man as "tall, dark haired, and very fit."

No, that couldn't be it at all. I chuckled to myself. I knew what it was like to be in a small town and have an interest in a handsome stranger. But that was a long time ago.

The paper hadn't been wrong, though. The Mystery Man certainly was all of those things.

And more.

CHAPTER TWO

Clare

W ITHIN TWO DAYS, the interest in the newest person in Hansonville had peaked and most people had moved on to other matters. That was the attention span in my little town. It was probably all for the better anyway since the poor guy had enough problems with not knowing who he was or how he'd come to town in the first place. The last thing he needed was a crowd of onlookers spying on him every minute of the day.

Even Laney fell out of love with the idea of the mysterious man pretty quickly. So much for fame, guy with amnesia.

The next time I went to the hospital to meet up with Emma it looked like it usually did—quiet and practically empty. She returned to her usual routine of working on the second floor after the crowds were sent on their way, happy to be back with the usual patients with hernias, gallbladder problems, and other sundry ailments that required a day or two stay in the general ward.

But as sometimes happened, just as I approached where she sat feverishly typing out her reports for the day before she could leave, a patient emergency sounded and every nurse on the floor raced to a room at the end of the hallway. Left to amuse myself until she returned, I sat down on a chair near the elevator and thumbed through an old, dog-eared issue of Glamour from 2013.

Ten minutes went by and I'd skimmed through all the must-know tips and techniques for the smoky eye and matte foundation look I'd never been able to master. I looked over at the table next to me and saw my only other choice in reading material was a slightly more recent Sports Illustrated from 2014 that looked like it had been rolled up and used to swat bugs and decided a walk might be better.

Not that I had anywhere to walk to. Roaming the halls of a hospital wasn't exactly interesting exercise. It felt like an invasion of privacy to look into patients' rooms as you passed by, but the only other choice was to stare straight ahead at the beige wall at each end of the hallway.

I began my stroll in the opposite direction of the emergency Emma and her co-workers had run to, trying to think of something other than how much the walls in this place needed some decorations. Even a few landscape pictures would be good. As it was, the second floor of Penn Valley Hospital had a dingy feel to it, like nobody had done anything with those beige walls since sometime before I was born.

Even though I tried not to look as I passed each room, I couldn't help it. Most of the rooms sat empty, thankfully, so I didn't feel like some creepy lurker as I slowly walked to the end of the long, dim hallway. Turning around, I looked up and saw the light in the ceiling had burned out, only adding to the dingy feeling. Somebody definitely needed to update this place.

I walked toward the nurses' station in the center of the hallway, happy for a brighter light for a few steps, but then it faded and became dimmer as I made my way toward the opposite end of the hallway. I turned my head to look at the room on the right and found it empty, but from the first room on the left someone called out and I spun around to see the mysterious stranger with amnesia staring out at me.

"Can you get me some water?" he asked in a frustrated tone that made the request sound more like an order. "I've been waiting for someone for nearly ten minutes."

I stared into his room and saw him sitting up with his arms folded across his sizeable chest I'd seen for a few moments the other day. Dressed in a light blue and white hospital gown, he looked far less impressive than he had shirtless as the doctor examined him in the ER, and now he had a look on his face that signaled his disgust with having to wait for a drink of water.

"They're working on someone at the end of the hallway. It sounded like an emergency," I explained, a little put out by his attitude, although I noted that even rude, he was definitely good looking.

"So I guess I'm going to have to get my own," he said, more frustrated than before.

He threw the sheet off his legs and spun himself so his feet hit the floor, but in just a second, his legs buckled. I ran into his room and grabbed him before he collapsed, barely able to hold his much larger frame up as he tried to stop himself from falling.

Helping him back into bed, I couldn't help notice he had great legs. Perfectly shaped, tanned, and muscular, they fit the rest of him I'd seen the other day. Whoever this guy was, he took care of himself before he ended up lying in the weeds on the side of Highway 27. He looked like he would be right at home on a beach somewhere.

A nude beach. In some exotic location where gorgeous people with beautiful bodies spread out sensually on the sand. Far away from Hansonville.

I found myself lost in thought imagining him

lying on that beach with those sexy legs and washboard abs slathered in oil and didn't realize he saw me staring at him until he cleared his throat.

"So, are you a nurse or just someone who likes to check out people at the hospital?" he asked, tearing me from the final remnants of my fantasy.

Looking up from his legs now covered by the sheet again, I shook my head far too quickly and felt my cheeks grow hot from embarrassment. "What? No. I mean…no, I'm not a nurse and no, I don't like to check people out. I'm here for something else entirely."

He smiled and tried not to laugh at my social clumsiness, but it was no use. Chuckling, he said, "Well, if you aren't either of those things, why were you looking into my room? Are you a patient? Do they have a psych floor and you got off it?"

"What? No!"

God, he was rude!

"Well, why were you looking in at me then?"

I didn't answer since I didn't have anything to say that didn't make me look like a fool. His smile faded away, and a darkness settled into his expression. "Are you another one of those reporters from the local yokel newspaper curious if I got my memory back or someone from the police to grill me for the hundredth time?"

Instantly, I became defensive. "No. I was just walking down the hall and you barked out that you wanted a drink. That's all."

He leaned back and sighed. "Oh. Well, okay."

I wanted to tell him to stick his attitude straight up his ass, but then I stopped myself. The guy was trapped in a hospital without any memory of who he was or what caused him to end up on the side of the road on the outskirts of a small town few people had ever heard of. No wonder he was cranky.

Not that he had to be nasty about things.

"I'll get a nurse for you now," I mumbled as I turned to leave.

"I'm sorry about thinking you were a nurse. In my defense, it was an honest mistake, don't you think?" he said, confusing me for a moment before I remembered that I was still dressed in my vet tech uniform.

Looking back at him, I smiled. "Yeah, I guess so."

He flashed me a smile that was a perfect mix of sexy and sincere, and for a moment I just stood there next to his bed staring at him. Dark-haired and fit. The newspaper had definitely gone with understatement this time. If I had to describe him, I would have said drop dead gorgeous with dark hair and eyes like a Greek god.

For the second time in five minutes, he caught

me lost in thought about him and asked, "So if you're not a nurse, why are you dressed like one?"

Once again embarrassed by the effect he had on me, I mumbled something about taking care of animals and then said, "I'll go get that nurse for you now. For the water. A drink of water."

Jesus, you'd think I never saw a good-looking man before in my life. I mean, he definitely didn't look like the local guys, but what was I thinking calling him a Greek god. Even if it was only to myself, what the hell was that about?

Ashamed at how I'd acted, I hurried out of his room and into the hall, where I ran headlong into Emma coming into his room. Stunned by seeing me there, she backed up and pointed at the door.

"What were you doing in there, Clare?"

"He wanted a drink. I was passing by and he asked me to get him a drink. He thought I was a nurse. Then his knees buckled…"

I was rambling, so I stopped myself and took a deep breath as Emma stared at me with a look of complete confusion. "Let me start over. I was just walking up and down the hall trying to kill time waiting for you. He saw me and asked me for a drink because he thought I was a nurse."

Looking down at my blue work uniform that resembled scrubs, I hoped she'd understand since none of what I was trying to say was making much sense. "I was just coming to find one of you guys."

She pulled me down the hall away from his room and whispered, "Did he talk to you?"

"Yeah. He asked for water. I just said that."

"Did he say anything else? What could you two have to talk about? He has amnesia," she said, looking back at his room with interest.

"I don't know how much he's supposed to know, but he understands being thirsty. I don't think you forget that even if you forget everything else. Why are you acting like this? I know I'm not supposed to go into patients' rooms, but you're acting weird."

She waved me off and said, "I'll be right back. I need to get him the water. Wait here."

In a flash, she rushed down the hall to get a pitcher and then hurried past me into his room. I watched her deliver it to him like he was some kind of dignitary, offering to pour him a cup and fawning all over him. I'd never seen Emma like that with anyone, patient or no patient.

Had she succumbed to being interested in him like everyone else had in town? They'd all moved on, leaving him behind like yesterday's news, but as I watched her flirt with him like it was Friday night at the local bar and she'd had a few too many drinks, I wondered if maybe she'd become infatuated with him too.

For his part, he sucked up the attention like a

sponge and appeared used to being adored. He merely sat back against the pillows and smiled at every compliment she gave him, looking perfectly content to let her continue falling over herself.

Not that I was very surprised. He was incredibly good looking with a great body and a very sexy smile and…

Oh, my God! I was no better than her. What kind of spell did this guy weave to get perfectly normal women to fall all over him?

I turned away from the show and headed back to the chair to flip through that old Sports Illustrated magazine. She followed a few seconds later and excitedly waved me over to the nurses' station.

"Isn't he charming?" she gushed like a teenage girl about the star quarterback of the Hansonville Trojans.

"Yeah, I guess, but what was with hitting on him like that? I'm surprised at you. You're usually all about being professional. He's good looking and all, but I thought at any moment you might jump into bed with him."

Another nurse walked by and Emma smiled at her before pushing me toward the alcove near the elevator. Looking down the hall toward his room she said in a hushed voice, "Do you know who that is?"

Now I was totally confused. What the hell was

she talking about? How would I know who he was if he didn't?

"Uh, no. He has amnesia, remember? Even he doesn't know who he is, Emma. What's gotten into you?"

With wide eyes, she said, "He's Marco Randolph, Clare."

She said that name like it should mean something to me. It didn't. I stared at her blankly. "Okay. So? Who's that?"

Sighing, she gave me a frustrated eye roll. "You know, if you didn't spend every night watching reruns of shows from the seventies, you'd know who Marco Randolph is. He's a movie star! A bona fide celebrity right here in Hansonville!"

"Celebrity? Him? I thought he had amnesia," I said as I peeked around the corner to look down the hall and saw two nurses hanging out near his room sneaking peeks in at him. "Who is he?"

Emma grabbed my arm and squeezed it in excitement. "I just told you. Marco Randolph! He's only the biggest up and coming star in Hollywood, and he's right here on my floor in my hospital. I can't believe it! We just found out a couple minutes ago after we finished working on Mr. Mendelsohn in 220. I nearly died when Karly told us."

"Up and coming, huh? What's he been in?

I've never heard of him before."

"Well, anyone who isn't doing their best Amish act knows who he is. Once word gets out, this floor is going to be ten times as bad as the ER was the other day," she said excitedly, like the idea of a mob suddenly didn't bother her so much anymore because he was a star.

"So he doesn't have amnesia after all, I guess, since everyone and their sister knows who he is."

Now I understood why he seemed right at home with her fawning over him. As an actor, he'd be accustomed to having that day and night.

"Wasn't he nice? I mean, for a movie star?" she said in a dreamy voice.

"I guess. For a movie star, I mean."

He hadn't been horrible. His attitude about the water was a little snappy, though.

As the news that the unknown man was some famous Hollywood bigwig sunk in, I had to admit a little disappointment that the mystery surrounding him had been solved. Very little in Hansonville wasn't what it seemed, perfectly understandable just from the surface, so not knowing anything about this stranger had been refreshing.

Well, so much for the intrigue. Now the crowds would return and Mr. Marco Randolph would have throngs of admirers around him again, just as I supposed he was used to.

"Give me five minutes and I'll be able to leave for lunch," Emma said as she smoothed her hair off her face.

As she headed toward his room again, she turned and said, "I just hope everyone else doesn't set up camp in his room. Karly already said she was calling her sister to come down. By the time I get back, there will probably be a line a mile long just to get into see him."

I chuckled at my friend being star struck and headed back to my chair and the old magazines near the elevator. Marco Randolph was a good-looking man, but now that I knew he was a movie star, even if he'd never been in anything I'd ever seen, I felt less impressed by his sexy smile and muscular body.

Hollywood stars weren't a good fit with small-town girls like me or Emma, no matter what the movies wanted us to believe. That smile and that body were carefully engineered to have exactly the effect they were having on every woman who came in contact with him, including me.

But I preferred someone more real, so Emma and his other fans could have him. I'd rather remain just as I'd been for a long time.

Single.

CHAPTER THREE

Matt

THE TALL, SKINNY doctor stood next to my bed looking at my chart and frowning, which only made his long face look even longer. Whatever he had to tell me wasn't good. After the excitement a few hours ago about me being Marco Randolph, I had hoped the news from that point on would be good. I was a big Hollywood star, so the expectation that things would at least improve from being a nobody found outside some town nobody knew about didn't seem like a huge leap of faith.

However, by the way Doctor Long Face was grimacing, something was definitely not okay.

"Well," he began and then cleared his throat as he squinted his eyes, "our examination of you has found nothing wrong with you, per se. You're physically in very good shape, and all your organs are working fine."

I threw back the sheet and moved to swing

my legs off the bed, careful to not have a repeat of what happened with that girl earlier or they'd keep me in this damn hospital for God only knew how long. The doctor stopped me with a hand on my shoulder, though, just as I moved to stand and shook his head.

"I'm sorry, but there's a problem."

Looking up at him, I asked, "What problem? You just said I'm fine, so I'd like to leave now, thank you."

He hesitated for a moment, and when he began to speak again, he stammered out the words, "Well, there's an issue with your identity."

I sat up straighter and looked him dead in the eye. "What the hell does it matter who I am if I'm well enough to walk out of this hospital? If you think I'm staying here for another night to enjoy whatever that shit was the cafeteria sent up yesterday, you're out of your mind. And what's the problem with my identity?"

"You're not Marco Randolph, Mr. Doe," he answered flatly.

Mr. Doe. We were back to that. "But…what do you mean? If I'm not, then what was all that about for the past few hours then? What makes you think I'm not Marco Randolph?"

The doctor's face grew long from a frown again. "The police contacted his manager in Los Angeles and she said the real Marco Randolph is fine. He's currently in the South of France on vacation after spending six months filming in Estonia."

"Estonia?" I said in stunned surprise.

"Yes. It's one of the Baltic States," the doctor explained unnecessarily as he began to search for information on his cell phone.

I pushed his hand away when he tried to show me on his phone a map of exactly where Estonia was located, disgusted by him and his news. "I don't need to know where goddamned Estonia is! Who gives a flying damn about that? What's going to happen to me now? I'm not staying here for another night!"

He continued to look at his phone, likely learning something he'd never known about Estonia, the fucking jewel of the Baltic, as I waited to hear what my fate would be. I had no intention of staying in this hospital for another hour of my life. There was nothing wrong with me.

At least nothing any of these people would be able to fix.

When he finally had satisfied himself with his knowledge of my new least favorite place in the world, Doctor Long face looked up from his phone and sighed. "Do you have any idea what you were doing out on Highway 27 the other day?"

My head began to throb at hearing that same damn question every single cop and doctor had asked me since the moment they brought me to this place. The answer wasn't going to change, so I couldn't imagine why they thought repeatedly asking the question was a good idea.

"No. I've told you and everyone else that about a million goddamned times! No! No! No! Would you like me to say it in another language? Maybe what they speak in freaking Estonia?" I said as I collapsed in frustration against the pillows behind me.

"If you only had even the faintest idea why you were there, maybe we could piece together what happened to you."

I doubted this guy or anyone in this town could piece together a kindergartener's puzzle, much less figure out something as intricate as a person's mind. As the pain behind my eyes began to settle into the rest of my head, I wondered if I'd ever get out of this hospital.

"Where exactly is there? Where am I?" I asked as I realized I didn't even know where there was.

"You're in Penn Valley Hospital in Hansonville, Pennsylvania about an hour west of Philly."

He said it with such pride you would have thought he was telling me I was in New York or Paris. Hansonville? Where the hell was that?

"Pennsylvania? I have no idea what I'd be doing out on that highway. I've never been to Pennsylvania before. Or at least I don't think I have. Maybe I have. I don't know."

Doing his best at showing some bedside manner, he touched me gently on the arm and said in a sympathetic voice, "Don't get upset. Most times, amnesia is only temporary. Patients sometimes just realize one day all their memories come back and then life goes on as normal. I'm sure that's what will happen for you too. You just have to give it time."

"How many patients have you seen that happen with?" I asked, for a moment wanting to believe the doctor in charge of my case had some knowledge of something that could help me.

And then he answered, and that hope was dashed.

Sheepishly, he said, "Well, none. You're our first ever case of amnesia here, but I've read about cases just like yours in the journals before."

It took every ounce of willpower I possessed not to snap back, "What journal? Ladies' Home Journal?" I didn't, though, choosing instead to just focus on when he planned to let me out of there so I could get on with my life. What I would do I had no idea, but I didn't plan on spending the rest of it there on the second floor of some Podunk hospital.

K.M. SCOTT

"I want to leave this place. When is that going to happen?" I asked, holding my frustration in as best I could, but it dripped off every word.

The doctor sighed heavily. "I don't feel right just turning you out into the streets not even knowing if you'll be okay, Mr. Doe."

Damnit, this guy actually thought he was going to keep me in this hospital until I got my memory back!

"Ask me whatever you want," I offered, relatively sure I could bluff my way through most of his simpleminded questions.

"What month is it?" he asked right away, leaning toward me eager to hear my answer.

Fuck. Why couldn't he ask me the year? That I knew. Turning my head to the left, I looked out the window and saw a bright and sunny day and green leaves on the trees.

"I'm thinking it's a good guess it's not December from what I know of the northeast in winter," I joked.

Pity filled the doctor's eyes. "What about the day? Do you know what day of the week it is?"

A smile crept onto my face. In my boredom, I'd listened to the nurses talk about their Friday night plans for hours as they milled about me when they thought I was Marco Randolph.

"Friday," I answered confidently. "See, I'm not entirely without an idea of what's going on."

"You still don't know your name, though," he said, ruining the good feeling I was experiencing.

"True, but the last name Doe isn't too bad. John Doe can work."

He looked at the top of my chart and then at me. "Actually, it's Matt Doe."

"What? Isn't it just customary for the name to be John?"

Smiling, he nodded. "It is, but someone obviously decided to go with Matt. You sort of look like a Matt, so I guess it can work if you're willing to go with it."

Christ. What kind of place had I been brought to where people didn't even follow basic common sense? Matt Doe? It was probably that nurse with the big boobs who kept sticking them in my face down in the ER when they brought me in. I wasn't sure if she planned to straddle me as I lay there on that gurney or actually treat me with how hard she was hitting on me.

Oh well. I could live with the name Matt. It could have been worse. She could have wanted to call me Marvin. Now that name would have to go.

"So, Matt, what will you do if I release you?"

Jesus, dealing with this guy was like riding an emotional rollercoaster. One minute he was dashing my hopes and then the next minute he made me think he may let me go.

I sat up straighter again, my spirits buoyed by the idea that I might finally get sprung from this place. "Well, I have a couple bucks in my pocket, I think, so maybe I'll just head on out of town and hope my memory comes back at some point."

Instantly, his bony shoulders sagged, telling me that I'd given the wrong answer. "I don't feel right just letting you wander around the country without knowing at least your real name before you go."

"But that could take weeks or months, couldn't it?" I asked in a panic. "You can't keep me in a hospital for that long. You guys have to have some rules that say if I don't have insurance or some way to pay that I can't stay. This is the United States, right?"

"Yes, but I can't in all good conscience just let you go, Mr. Doe. I mean, if you were a local resident, at least I'd be able to keep an eye on you for a few weeks to make sure you're okay, but if you're just going to leave town and wander around the world, I won't know what happens to you."

"Then I can stay in this town. What is it called again? Hansonville? I can stay in Hansonville until my memory comes back. I have a few bucks. I can find a room someplace. Whatever it takes, Doc. I just can't stay in this hospital for another day. I'm going stir crazy here!"

He narrowed his eyes to slits and sighed again. "Hmmmm…I did hear just this morning that Sarah over at the Colonial Inn is looking for a handyman. Do you think you could fix things?"

I didn't bother to remind him that I had amnesia so any memory of my being able to fix things wasn't readily available at the moment. I just smiled and nodded. "Look at me. I have to be able to fix stuff, don't you think?"

"Well, she might be willing to provide you a room if you helped her around the inn. Maybe if you can't fix things you can do chores like mow the lawn and trim the hedges. I don't think she has a gardener on staff since Joe usually does those things for her."

"Great! Joe deserves a few days off, whoever he is. All you have to do is give me my walking papers and I'll head right on over to the Colonial Inn."

"Joe is her husband, and you're right. He really does deserve some time off. He's been working too hard since his heart attack last spring," the doctor explained, as if I knew who he was talking about or even cared.

"Terrific!"

I moved to get out of the bed and began walking toward the chair in the corner where one of the nurses had carefully folded my clothes.

"You get whatever paperwork you need ready, and I'll get dressed. It looks like someone was even nice enough to wash my clothes. Even better."

"Wait! Wait!" he said, grabbing my arm as the back of my hospital gown flew open. "We need to talk about your amnesia more."

I slipped one leg into my jeans and sat down on the chair. Looking up at him, I saw he was serious. "What else is there to say? I don't have a memory of anything before the other day. You said it will come back at some point, so I just have to wait. In the meantime, since you want me around so you can check up on me, I'll be at the Colonial Inn, assuming this Sarah person is willing to give me a job and let me stay there."

Worry etched into his long face, he said in a somber voice, "The human brain is a tricky thing. It can decide it doesn't want to deal with something one day and then the memories are gone. They can come back or they may not. Your mind might be intentionally keeping you from remembering who you are because of some traumatic experience."

I stood up and buttoned my jeans before tossing the hospital gown onto the bed. "Well, I'm not going far, so if my brain decides to let my memories come rushing back, I promise you'll be the first person I tell. Good enough?"

He hemmed and hawed about the brain being

a delicate organ as I slid my black T-shirt over my head. Whatever he said, I'd agree to, just as long as I got to leave this goddamned hospital.

Lowering myself back down into the chair, I put my socks and boots on and looked up to read his name tag. Dr. Franklin Connors.

"Doctor Connors, I promise I'll be careful. I'm just going to be here in town, so what could be better? If I remember anything, I'll call you first. Deal?"

I stood up ready to leave, but he wasn't finished with me just yet. Still looking far too worried for the situation, he furrowed his brow and said, "Just don't overdo it, Mr. Doe. You never know when your memories will return, and it might be quite traumatic when they do."

This guy was all about the trauma, but I knew I had to put his fears to rest to get out, so I patted his shoulder and smiled. "Please, call me Matt. I promise you, Doctor Connors, that I won't overdo anything. I'll help Sarah over at the Colonial Inn so you can keep an eye on me, and when I remember who I am, I'll go back to my life. It'll be fine. You'll see."

"I hope so. You seem like a nice person, Matt. I'd hate to see you end up unhappy when your memory returns."

"No need to worry, Doc. Hansonville seems like a nice place, so I'm sure I'll be more than fine.

Just think of it as a little vacation, like my brain decided one day that I needed a break. What better place to do that than in a town like this?"

He wholeheartedly agreed that his home town was wonderful and just the kind of place where a person could take a break from the hustle and bustle of the world. As he walked out to the nurses' station to get my discharge papers, I couldn't help but agree with him.

Hansonville would be perfect for me. At least until I got my head together, and who knew how long that would take.

CHAPTER FOUR

Clare

THE FOURTH OF July red, white, and blue bunting still hung from the telephone poles across Main Street, making the town look like it was always waiting for a parade to start. The garbage crew, which doubled as the holiday decorations crew year-round and then tripled as the snow removal crew in the winter, would get to taking them down sometime in late August just before they had to hang the Labor Day decorations, which looked very much the same as the ones they were removing. As I walked by, I wondered if anyone had ever suggested to the town council that maybe just keeping the same patriotic decorations up May through September would be a better idea.

Summer in Hansonville always seemed slower than any other time of the year. Not that my hometown ever reached a point where things moved quickly. It never ceased to amaze me that we were barely an hour away from Philly, yet it seemed like we were lightyears behind there when it came to most things.

For God's sake, we just got a Starbucks less than six months ago, and when it opened, everyone worried that the Patriot Restaurant would suddenly go out of business because of the competition. It didn't, and as I looked across the street toward the red brick building that housed it, I had to admit I was happy about their ability to co-exist with the new, sexy coffee shop in town. Yes, the trading on the whole colonial thing was a little hokey with their servers dressed in period garb to look like Betsy Ross and Paul Revere and their refusal to use anything but metal plates for food, but the place did serve the best strawberry shortcake east of the Mississippi.

Or so they claimed.

But since I'd never left the state of Pennsylvania and had only been to Philly a handful of times, perhaps I wasn't a worthy judge of that claim. No matter. It still was a dessert everyone in town raved about at one time or another.

As I stared at the restaurant lost in thought, I noticed someone sitting at one of the tables the Patriot liked to set up to make it seem like a café. Training my gaze on them, I saw the man who had showed up three weeks ago on Highway 27 who everyone had thought was that famous movie star for about fifteen minutes. Emma told me all about how disappointed the entire nursing staff at the hospital had been when they found out that Marco Randolph guy was nowhere close to Hansonville and instead lounging on the beach on the French Riviera.

Surprised to see him, I wondered why he was still in town. Even if he wasn't a famous actor, he had to have better things to do than hang out in Hansonville.

People stared at him as they walked by on that side of the street, and part of me felt bad for him. He may not have been from here, but that was no reason to gawk at the guy.

Had he gotten his memory back? I quickly dismissed that idea. If he had remembered who he was, he probably wouldn't be sitting outside the Patriot Restaurant drinking a cup of coffee in the middle of the afternoon in mid-July.

As a group of older women stopped a few feet away from him and pointed in his direction, I considered crossing the street to speak to him, but then the women all sat down at the table with him and I realized no one was being rude to him. They seemed to actually know him.

I'd lived in Hansonville all my life and no one would approach me if I sat outside on Main Street. He'd been here for less than a month and already had the older ladies in town all over him.

That whole not being a famous movie star thing hadn't hurt him, it appeared.

As the women chatted him up, he waved at me and smiled. Caught off guard, I quickly waved back and hurried on my way down the street back toward the vet's office.

Behind me, I heard someone yell something, and when I turned around, I saw the guy with amnesia walking toward me. He flashed me another of those perfect smiles and waved his hand at me like he wanted me to stop.

What in the world would he have to say to me?

"Hey, uh...I don't think I know your name, but would you stop for a second?" he called to me in a voice that surprised me at how deep it was.

Slowing down, I let him catch up with me in front of Carson's Florist, and I pretended to admire one of their gorgeous flower baskets with purple and pink petunias that tumbled out of their container, hanging in long trails toward the ground. Out of the corner of my eye, I saw the guy wearing a look like he really had something to discuss with me.

He stopped next to me and shook his head. "I think I might be a little out of shape."

I tried to be subtle as I scanned his body, instantly deciding he was in fantastic shape just as he was when I saw him in the hospital. His jeans fit perfectly, accentuating those great legs and a nice ass, and his T-shirt hugged his muscular chest and arms like a second skin.

Oh, no, I have to disagree, sir. You're in perfect shape.

Suddenly uncomfortable like I'd been that day in his hospital room when he caught me checking him out, I began walking again before he even had a chance to say another word. For some reason, he made me nervous. Who knew anything about this guy? He could be an ax murderer.

"Hey, wait up! I wanted to talk to you!" he called after me.

"Oh? What about?" I asked as I continued to walk down the sidewalk.

"Well, how have you been?" he asked while I looked in the front window of Baker's Confectioners at an adorable yellow cake in a shape of a hunk of Swiss cheese with a tiny, grey candy mouse peeking out of one of the holes. They always showcased their most interesting creations in the front window, and today was no exception.

"Fine," I muttered before moving further down the store window to look at a three-tiered white frosted cake with purple flowers draped around the sides like a frosting garland.

"That's good. In the market for a cake?

Having a party, or is it your birthday? If so, happy birthday," he said in a chipper voice.

I turned to look at him and shook my head. "No, it's not my birthday. I just like to look in the display window. I have to go now."

Pushing past him, I continued down the sidewalk, a little faster now, past Baker's next-door neighbor, Gifts by Fancy, a specialty shop for unique items. Fancy, whose real name was Francine but everyone called her Fancy since she was a little girl, had a knack for finding the most interesting things from all around the world. Whenever anyone in Hansonville wanted something out of the ordinary, they went to Fancy's store.

In her front window, a peacock carved out of teakwood stared out at me, and behind it stood Fancy herself smiling and waving enthusiastically. I looked to my right and saw the guy next to me waving back.

Damn. Did he know everybody in town already?

I stepped around him and began walking quickly, no longer paying any attention to the shop windows. All I wanted to do was get away from him, even though I had to admit that he was good looking and smelled great. So few men wore cologne anymore, and it was a nice change from the usual guys in town.

But that didn't mean I wanted to hang out and chat with him.

"What have you been up to since I saw you last?" he asked as he stayed step for step with me.

I looked over at him and once again saw that gorgeous smile. I wouldn't have been surprised if he was able to charm the birds out of the trees with it. His dark eyes stared down at me intently, like he really wanted to hear the answer to his question of what I'd been up to.

"I've been getting to know the town and the people here," he said, almost like answering his own question. "They've been really nice. It's pretty quiet, as far as towns go, but then again, I'm not really an expert on towns."

"I guess," I said as I continued walking, concerned that he actually had suffered a head injury that day out on Highway 27 with the way he was talking what sounded like gibberish.

"But all in all, it's been pretty good. I'm staying at the Colonial Inn and helping Sarah out with some handyman work there so Joe can rest. He shouldn't be doing so much anyway since he's still recuperating from his heart attack."

His talking about townspeople like he knew them all his life made me stop dead, and I turned to face him. He smiled in anticipation of me finally engaging with him.

"Do you know everyone in Hansonville

already? Didn't you just roll into town a few weeks ago?" I asked, far more sharply than I'd intended.

My tone surprised him, and he leaned away from me like he expected to get hit. "Yeah, well, I guess."

"I guess. Well, I have to get going. Nice chatting."

I left him standing there in front of Kendra's Hair Salon and crossed the street to head toward my car parked at the vet's. Without looking back, I thought I'd shaken him, but I was wrong. Just as I stepped onto the curb on the other side of Main Street, he jumped in front of me, forcing me to stop.

"Hey, did I do something wrong? I don't think I did, although I'm not sure if the amnesia affects things after the accident or just before," he said as he looked at me with hurt in his eyes.

Damn. I really had been rude to him, hadn't I? All he seemed to want to do was talk. In fact, he'd been nothing but nice. I just couldn't shake the fact that he made me uneasy. Maybe it was because he was so damn charming. He really was good looking, and something about that unnerved me. Dark hair, dark eyes that a woman could get lost in, and a body that didn't quit. He may not have been a movie star, but he could have been with a face like that.

Smiling, I said, "I'm sorry if I was being rude. I just think if you're going to be hanging out in Hansonville you probably should avoid being friends with me. I'm sort of an outcast around here."

I had no idea why I said that. It wasn't a lie or anything, but I'd never admitted that to anyone, even Emma. Did this guy have a way of hypnotizing me to reveal my deepest, darkest secrets?

Just another reason to avoid him.

"No way. I can't believe that. You've been nice to me every time we've talked, even when I was being a presumptuous ass in the hospital."

"It isn't about being nice or not. That's not the issue."

"Then what is it?" he asked, clearly not understanding my point.

Looking around at the people walking down the sidewalk toward us, I studied them as I always did and tried to think of a way to explain what I meant. They looked just like me in their shorts and T-shirts and smiled as they approached us. Nobody in town had ever been nasty or cruel to me. In fact, when my father died, the citizens of Hansonville turned out in droves to his funeral, even people I knew had never spent a moment's time with him.

No, it wasn't that they disliked me. It was

something subtler.

I looked back at him and took a deep breath, letting it out slowly. "I'm different from the rest of the people here. It's okay. I've always been like this. I just figure that you should probably want to find someone else to talk to."

He smiled as the people passed us and said hello before turning back to face me. "I don't see it, unless you mean how beautiful you are. Then I can definitely see how you're different from everyone else in town. But that's a good thing and no reason for me to not want to talk to you."

Oh, he absolutely could charm the birds out the trees.

"Are you always this smooth?" I asked, feeling my cheeks warm as I blushed from his compliment.

He chuckled and shook his head. "I think you mean sincere, and yes, I am. Or I think I am. I'm not sure."

"You're not sure if you were being sincere when you told me I was beautiful?"

"No, that's not what I meant. Maybe I should start over. Hi, my name is Matt. What's yours?" he asked as he extended his hand to shake mine.

"You got your memory back?" I asked, surprised he knew his name.

He smiled and shook his head. "No. That was the name on the chart in the hospital. Matt Doe."

I took his hand in mine and felt its strength as I shook it. "Well, Matt, I'm Clare Schiffer."

"Nice to meet you, Clare. So now that you and I know each other so well, will you have dinner with me?" he asked, full of that sexy charm that seemed to come from him so easily.

"No, but at least the next time I see you in the street I'll know your name," I said with a chuckle as I stepped around him and began to walk away.

He didn't follow me that time, and I had to admit I was a little disappointed. If I was being honest, I did like him. What wasn't to like? He was good looking, charming, and sexy as all hell. On top of that, he oozed confidence, even though he still had no idea who he was or where he came from.

And right there lay the problem. He had amnesia. The man had no idea of anything before three weeks ago when he turned up on the side of Highway 27. For all anyone knew, including me, he could be some escaped convict. Or some no good drifter.

Or a married man with a wife, two kids, and a cockapoo named Waggles.

What would happen when his memory of whatever his life had been finally came back to him? No doubt, he'd leave Hansonville, understandably. This wasn't his home. Somewhere out in the world, he had a life, and whether that life included a family or even just a few close friends, he wouldn't want to stay here.

My past was littered with love affairs gone bad. In fact, in some ways I envied Matt. I'd love to be able to forget those heartbreaks. But I couldn't, and they warned me that getting involved with a man who belonged somewhere else and maybe to someone else wasn't what I needed in my life.

CHAPTER FIVE

Matt

CLARE TURNED THE corner and disappeared from view, but she hadn't dampened my interest in any way with her brush off. Her warm brown hair that touched just below her shoulders and made me want to run my fingers through it was just one part of her that I liked. Those intense blue eyes that always seemed to look at me with suspicion intrigued me, and something about the way her clothes gave a hint at the body underneath made me want to know more.

Much more.

I didn't know what the hell she was talking about when she said she was different, other than how stunning she was compared to every other woman in this town. I had to admit, though, that I couldn't help but wonder and since I had nothing but time on my hands, I wasn't about to give up on getting her to at least go out to dinner with me.

I headed back to my table outside the Patriot Restaurant to formulate a plan to get her to say yes to a first date. No doubt I'd be able to convince her to go out on a second and then a third, but I knew that first date would be the most challenging one to get her to agree to.

Not that I wasn't up to it. Life in Hansonville bordered on non-existent, and in the three weeks since I came to town, I'd found little to challenge me. Sarah handed me a list of chores each morning that I had to do around the Colonial Inn, and I did them, usually as slowly as possible so I could drag them out all day. If not, I ended up sitting around twiddling my thumbs for hours, something a lot of people seemed content to do in this town.

Boredom usually set in by lunchtime, and by late afternoon every day, I had to wrestle with my conscience and not walk straight out of town on the highway where they'd found me almost a month ago. I'd given Doctor Connors my word that I'd stay in town until my memory returned, though, and since I still didn't have even the faintest idea who I was, where I was from, or what kind of past I had, for the time being, I'd stay in Hansonville.

So while I had to be here, I figured I might as well make the best of it, and what better use of my time could there be than getting a date with Clare

Schiffer?

Taking my seat at the table in front of the Patriot like I did every afternoon, I thought about how I'd get her to say yes to me. She had more than a healthy dose of distrust for men, it seemed. Likely some local yokel dickhead had cheated on her with a girl who worked doubles at the convenient mart on the edge of town. I could see it as clear as day. His name was probably something like Jim Bob or Floyd and the girl's name was Dixie or something equally as stupid.

Asshole.

They probably snuck around behind her back for a few months while she walked around town thinking she'd found the man of her dreams. Oh yeah. That's what happened. Meanwhile, Mr. Small-Town Douche and Trashy Side Chick were off banging like a broken screen door.

Well, the ghost of whatever had happened wasn't going to stand in my way. I had mystery on my side, and if I'd learned anything in my time around Hansonville, it was that mystery was a commodity that was nearly priceless. Probably because the place was as boring as watching paint dry.

"Excuse me. We saw you here and wondered if you're that guy from the highway," a voice said next to my left ear.

I turned to see a relatively attractive woman

with blond hair and at least C cups and her cute but nearly flat-chested friend staring at me wide-eyed. See what I meant about mystery? These people ate this shit up. Got to love small towns, although calling someone that guy from the highway after he was found lying in a stretch of weeds wasn't exactly sweet.

Turning on the charm, I smiled and nodded. "I am. They call me Matt. Who might you be?" I asked with a wink.

The friend wasted no time in pulling up a chair to sit down, and the woman who asked me who I was followed suit. Eager to chat, they both began to speak at the same time and then laughed when they realized I couldn't understand a thing coming out of their mouths.

"We're sorry. It's just so interesting, you know? I mean, your story. First, you were a total mystery, and then we all thought you were Marco Randolph, and then we found out you weren't him, even though you're the spitting image of him. The spitting image indeed. I'm Janine, and this is Stacy."

I extended my hand to shake Janine's very delicate hand and wondered if those breasts on display were just for me or if everyone in town got the full cleavage treatment. "It's so nice to meet you, Janine."

"We aren't bothering you, are we?" Stacy

asked as she thrust her hand out to push her friend's away.

"Nope. Just enjoying a wonderful summer afternoon in beautiful Hansonville," I said with a smile as I spread my arms out wide.

Both women grinned as they let their gazes travel over my torso. I didn't need to know a damn thing about anything in the past to know they liked what they saw too.

Janine inched her chair closer to mine and touched my bicep as I lowered my arms to my sides. "Can I ask if you've remembered anything yet? It must be so terrible not to remember a thing about your life. I can't even imagine," she cooed.

I shook my head and sighed like the sad soul they assumed I was. "Not a thing yet. I'm trying not to think about it too much, you know? I just want to live in the here and now."

Janine and Stacy sighed. That phrase—live in the here and now—had some kind of magical properties to it that made women around here turn into putty in men's hands. Well, at least my hands. I had no idea why since it meant next to nothing to me, but every time I uttered those words to a female in this town, they practically melted right in front of me.

"That's such an incredible way to approach life," Stacy said in dreamy voice as she stared into my eyes like they held the answer to some singular question she'd been asking all her life. "I just love that."

"Me too," Janine said as her gaze settled on my face. "It's just so positive and affirming."

I didn't bother to clue them into the fact that a man with amnesia who couldn't remember anything before three weeks ago didn't have much choice but to live in the here and now. That's all there was. It wasn't some kind of spirituality I possessed.

But I had no problem with milking it for my own benefit.

"Well, each one of us has to do our best to make all we can out of the cards we're dealt."

Both women's eyes opened wide in awe of my Zen-like acceptance of having nothing to fall back on besides the last twenty-one days. Well, that and their happiness at touching my biceps and shoulders. That was another thing about this place. Everyone touched me, especially the women. Even the old women ran their hands up and down my arms when they talked to me.

Almost everyone.

Clare seemed to be the odd exception. She not only didn't touch me but seemed to want to flee every time I was nearby. I would have dismissed any thought of being with her because of that if it wasn't for the fact that she also seemed to get lost in thought whenever I was around too, and when

I noticed, she always blushed.

I loved that. Her cheeks got pink, and then as soon as she felt herself blushing, she turned away. It had a charm to it that seemed old-fashioned, even among all the people in Hansonville, a place time appeared to have forgotten.

I wanted to see more of that, preferably when the two of us were alone. And naked. Definitely naked.

To that end, I wondered if Janine and Stacy might know something about Clare that could help me.

"So, tell me, ladies, what's it like around here? Everyone seems really nice. Is it really that way? There's got to be some dirt on someone in Hansonville," I said with a wink.

"I wish!" Janine said, punctuating her desire by trailing her fingertips over my shoulder.

"It's so boring around here," Stacy whined as she squeezed my forearm. "There's no dirt anywhere. Nobody does anything even slightly risqué here."

"Well, everyone has been so incredibly nice to me, especially since I'm so new in town. I mean, every single person has been so wonderful."

I paused a moment for effect and continued. "Well, that's not entirely true. Everyone except that girl Clare, that is. She doesn't seem to like me," I said, intentionally leading them to the subject I wanted to discuss.

"Clare? Do you mean Clare Schiffer? She's sort of different," Stacy said with a grimace that made her face look like a sock puppet's.

"Well, I don't know what's so different about her, but I get the feeling she doesn't like me much. I was sort of rude when I met her in the hospital, and I guess first impressions are definitely lasting ones with her."

"I wouldn't worry about her. She doesn't bother with many town events. She came to the Fourth of July picnic and spent all her time reading a book. Who does that?" Janine said in disbelief, as if reading in public places was equal to an unbelievable breach of public ethics.

Stacy slapped her playfully and giggled. "She's just quiet, I think. I heard a rumor a while back that she and some guy were hot and heavy and ready to get married, but then he just vanished from town one day. Practically left her standing at the altar."

Undeterred by her friend's chastising, Janine added, "Maybe she's quiet because she's a serial killer and she hacked him up with an ax and buried his body parts around her property. You know what they say about the quiet ones. Still waters run deep and dirty."

They laughed at the idea of some poor guy's body parts strewn about Clare's yard like they'd just heard the joke of the century. Definitely macabre and definitely not my style, but they seemed to like talking about Clare, so I pushed them for more information.

"No way," I said, forcing a smile. "I haven't seen a yard in this town big enough to bury a man."

"Oh no, she doesn't live in Hansonville center. She lives outside of town out on Highway 27," Stacy explained, giving me just what I needed to know.

"Yeah, that's how she could get away with it. Who knows? Maybe she lured him out to that house of hers and when he told her he didn't want to marry her anymore, she chopped his head off. Once that's done, I imagine it's not much to just keep chopping things up until someone's all gone," Janine said with a look of interest like she'd thought about the subject at length.

"There would be a ton of blood, though, wouldn't there?" Stacy asked me, as if I'd know how much blood would spill from a human body when it was chopped up.

"I'd guess," I said forcing yet another smile but tired of the conversation since I'd learned all I could from them. Their gossipy bullshit wouldn't help me in any real way in my quest to get Clare, but their telling me where she lived would.

Before they could start talking again, I stood

from the table and gathered up my coffee cup. "I wish I could sit here all day and talk with you two, but duty calls at the Colonial Inn and I wouldn't want to disappoint my boss after she was so sweet to give me a job to tide me over."

Both Stacy and Janine stared up at me with disappointed faces. They had no idea how much I wanted to get away from them and their grisly sense of humor. Clare may have been different, but I had to wonder if that was such a bad thing, after all.

"We'll have to do this again," they said in unison.

With a wink, I turned to head back into the restaurant. "Absolutely, ladies. I look forward to it."

I snuck out the side door and headed straight toward Highway 27. Curiosity not about some dead boyfriend in pieces around Clare's yard but about where she lived filled my mind. Did she live alone or with family? I hadn't seen a wedding band on her left ring finger, so I'd assumed she was single, even if she had a standoffish way about her.

Maybe I'd been reading the vibe coming off her all wrong.

Before I made it even half a mile in the scorching July sun, a truck pulled up beside me at the edge of town. I looked in and saw one of the older nurses from the hospital who'd worked on the second floor. Tandy had been one of the sweetest people during my time there. Grey-haired with soft blue eyes, she looked worried to see me walking on the side of the road.

Leaning over, she lowered the window and flashed me a toothy smile. "Hey, you! Where you going? Want a ride?"

I walked up to the side of her truck and put my head through the window. With a smile, I said, "You shouldn't be picking up strange men on the side of the road."

She waved away my concern and opened the door for me. "This is Hansonville. Nobody's a stranger here. Get in and I'll take you where you're going."

Taking her up on her offer, I jumped into the truck and we took off down the road. Tandy hummed some country tune for a minute or so before turning the music down and looking over at me.

"Where you off to today?"

I knew I couldn't just tell her I was doing some reconnaissance to find out all I could about Clare, so I smiled and hurried to think of another answer. "I thought I'd take a stroll out to the place where they found me to see if it jogs any memories, you know?"

She didn't question what I said for a second. I guessed it sounded perfectly normal for someone with amnesia to do something like that.

Personally, I had not one damn inkling of interest in seeing that spot on the side of the road where I'd opened my eyes one day three weeks ago to find myself in some strange town without a clue as to who I was or what I was doing there.

I'd remember who I was sooner or later. Until then, I planned on using my time in Hansonville to the fullest extent, and that meant finding a way to get Clare Schiffer to go out on a date with me.

That's all it would take. I didn't know why, but I didn't care to think too deeply about that either.

"Sounds like a good idea to me," Tandy said in that sweet, grandmotherly tone she'd used ever since the first moment we met in the hospital. "Have you had any flashes of anything that would help you figure out who you are?"

I shook my head. "Not a one. All I know is that I'm Matt and I live and work at the Colonial Inn. I've got a pretty short history to memorize."

She chuckled and reached out to squeeze my arm. "It'll be okay. You've got a great attitude toward the whole thing. That's important. No use in pushing yourself. It's going to happen when it happens. In the meantime, I'm happy to see that you're enjoying your time in Hansonville. We're a pretty good lot around here, so I had a feeling you'd be okay."

As we turned onto Highway 27, I paid attention so I'd be able to get back to town when

I wanted to. Near the intersection of Main Street and the highway and almost entirely hidden by overgrown bushes stood a sign that said, "Leaving Hansonville. Hope to see you soon!"

Tandy noticed the sign too and remarked with a laugh, "We don't want anyone to leave, so we hide that."

"From what I see, no one seems to leave Hansonville. Everyone I've met has lived here all their life."

She looked over at me and nodded. "It's that kind of place. We have very little crime, decent schools, good people. What more could you ask for?"

I nodded in return as I thought of a number of things I would ask for in town. Another restaurant besides the Patriot. Something to stay open past midnight. A couple more places to get a drink.

But I didn't say any of that to Tandy. She clearly loved Hansonville, and she had every right to. It was her home. And she'd been nice enough to give me a ride, so she didn't deserve me rattling off ways I thought the place could be improved.

"You're right about the good people. I can't say enough about how nice everyone has been to me since I got to town. I know at first they thought I was that movie star guy, but even now, everyone smiles when they see me and waves hello as I meet them on the street."

Puffing out her chest with pride in her hometown, Tandy smiled. "See what I mean? Hansonville is a great place to live."

I had a feeling someone like Tandy might be able to give me some good information on Clare, so I waited a moment before saying in a sad voice, "Well, not everyone. There's this one person who doesn't seem to like me much at all."

Tandy's head snapped around toward me, and she looked shocked. "Who? I can't imagine who would be like that in my town."

"It's not that big a deal. I just wonder what I did to offend her," I said with my best concerned look in my eyes.

Clutching the steering wheel tightly in anger, Tandy asked, "Is its old Mrs. Janson? I tell you, that woman could make the good Lord himself want to smack her. I saw her coming out of Baker's the other day and I could have sworn when I looked in Mrs. Baker was crying. Don't you let that old bag get to you, son. She's just one, thank God."

In the three weeks since I'd come to Hansonville, I'd never met anyone named Mrs. Janson, and it sounded like I'd been lucky not to. Nothing like being berated by some old woman to ruin a guy's day.

"No, no. It's not her. It's a woman named Clare Schiffer. For the life of me, I can't figure out why every time I see her, she either turns away like I'm a leper or scowls right in my face."

I knew that was laying it on a little thick. Clare hadn't really been anything but aloof, but I wouldn't learn anything telling Tandy that, so I embellished a little in the name of romance.

"Oh, Clare. She's not so bad. She's just a little unapproachable, I guess. Her father was like that too."

"Was?" I asked, instantly interested in her use of the past tense to describe him.

"Yeah. He passed away a few years ago. One day he was fine and heading off to work, and the next day he was dead."

"Oh," I said quietly, sorry to hear Clare had lost her father.

Tandy looked over at me and nodded like she too felt sorry for her. "He liked to keep to himself like his daughter, and ever since his death, she's been pretty scarce around town, for the most part. She still lives in the family house right down the road here."

"I had no idea, but then again, since I have no idea of who I am or what my life was like before three weeks ago, I guess I couldn't, right?" I said with a smile, doing my best to be self-effacing.

Pulling the car over to the side of the road, Tandy shifted into park and pointed out the window. "I think that's where they found you, isn't it?"

I looked out the window at the high grass and

overgrown bushes and immediately recognized that as the place where I'd begun my life in Hansonville. "Yeah, that's it."

"Are you going to be okay to get back to the inn?" she asked as I began to open the door.

"Yeah, I'll be fine."

She peered out the front window and pointed up at the sky. "Remember that storms tend to roll in fast on these summer afternoons. You won't have to worry too much, though. Just find an old barn or shed and wait it out. They usually pass as quickly as they come."

"Okay, sounds good. Thanks again for the ride and the company, Tandy," I said as I got out of the truck. Looking up, I saw nothing but a blue cloudless sky and the sun beating down on me.

"Anytime, hon. Take care, and when you're in the neighborhood, stop in at the hospital and say hi! Everyone would love to see you again."

"I will. Thanks again, Tandy."

I watched her drive off and took a deep breath to fill my lungs with hot summer air. I hadn't had any interest whatsoever in seeing this spot, so I quickly began to walk down the road toward where I hoped to find Clare's house. As much as I would have liked Tandy's sudden rainstorm to happen, it didn't look like I'd get any relief from the heat anytime soon.

Hopefully, Clare's house wasn't too far away.

CHAPTER SIX

Matt

AFTER WALKING FOR about half a mile, I saw a big white farmhouse on the right side of the road and silently thanked God because with every step it seemed to get hotter, if that was possible. The house looked exactly like the kind I imagined Clare would live in.

A large, wraparound porch on the front gave it a friendly look, and the swing to the right of the front door made the place look downright homey. An old house, it seemed to only slightly mask the huge backyard behind it. I wasn't good at eye balling acres, but it had to be at least five. The paint was a little worn and could have dealt with a touch up, but it only served to make the house look more welcoming somehow.

That description didn't actually fit with how she'd behaved toward me on either occasion, but I had a sense Clare was nicer than she let on. At least I hoped she was. It would be a big disappointment to find out she was nothing but a nice-looking face and body. I mean, as far as men went, I guessed I could be pretty shallow, not that I knew from any experience other than the past few weeks, but that didn't mean I wanted some harpy, no matter how hot she looked.

I wasn't getting the sense Clare was that, though. I felt from her a warmness I suspected lay buried beneath the surface. It seemed like if I could just break through that hardened exterior of hers that I could find it.

Looking around, something about the big oak tree in the front yard made the entire scene feel like something from one of the postcards the Colonial sold in the lobby. I liked that. It gave me hope that behind the defensiveness, I'd find a sweetness in her.

A silver car parked in the dirt driveway next to the house told me she was home, so I hurried to behind the huge trunk of the oak tree so I could get a better look at the place. I made it there just in time as that storm Tandy had predicted seemed to come out of nowhere and suddenly rain poured out of the sky like someone had turned on a spigot.

Clare walked around the house closing windows as the storm moved in with thunder and lightning. Two loud claps rattled the air around me, and I crouched down against the tree hoping to keep dry. I peeked around it and watched her take a seat in the front window and gaze out at the horrible weather like it brought her some happiness. The corners of her mouth hitched up into a tiny smile that made her even more beautiful than before. I sat mesmerized just looking at her enjoy the storm as it raged around me, forgetting for a moment that I was sitting in the middle of it.

Another loud clap of thunder brought me back to reality and startled her, so she sat back away from the window and looked out from a safer distance. I liked this version of Clare. This girl had a calmness that I hadn't seen in her before. I wondered what she was thinking about as she stared out at the black clouds and jagged white streaks of lightning that lit up the darkened sky.

She lived alone, without even a dog or cat, from what I could see. I had a feeling those two gossipy women from the Patriot Restaurant would have been scared shitless to be out here alone in a storm.

But not Clare. She just continued to sit near the window, back a little closer now that the storm had begun to move out, and watched nature do its thing all around her house.

The more I saw of her, the more beautiful she became. Why did she live alone then? Maybe she was an ax murderer like those two women had claimed. Maybe that fiancé of hers in fact was scattered around her property like a macabre reminder of what he tried to do to her.

I shook my head to rid it of that nonsense. Clare was no more an ax murderer than I was. Not that I knew for sure I wasn't, but I had a feeling I was a decent guy. At least decent enough not to kill someone and stash their remains in holes around my house.

No, Clare wasn't an ax murderer. She was just a woman who seemed to have developed a distinct dislike for me, even though I had no idea why.

I planned on overcoming that obstacle, though. I had no idea what my track record with the fairer sex looked like, but I knew one thing. Clare would be a challenge, but I was up to it. So she had a headstrong thing about her? No problem. I could handle it.

I just needed to find a way to get close enough to her to show her that. I didn't know what it was going to take, but if I was up to the challenge of regaining my own identity, I could handle getting to know a beautiful woman. Somehow that felt easier.

In a haze of thoughts and ideas about her, I walked back into town in the afternoon heat that seemed even worse after that sudden storm. And more humid. The rain had turned the air into something akin to soup.

As I made my way through quaint Hansonville, I searched my mind for some kind of clue to where I was supposed to be at that moment in the world, but it only served to frustrate me. It was as if my mind drew a blank every time I tried to remember anything before three weeks ago.

Passing the hospital, I saw Tandy leaning up against the side of the wall chatting to some guy in overalls. When I entered her field of vision, she waved at me and called out, "Hey! Come here!"

I nodded and quickly picked up my pace to approach them. "Twice in one day," I said with a smile. "People are going to start talking."

"Second time in one afternoon," she replied with a hearty laugh. Nudging the man in the side, she said, "This is the guy I told you about, John."

The man smiled and gave me a nod. "It's nice to meet you, Matt. I'm John. Heard you're in a bit of a situation, huh?"

A heavy-set guy with five o'clock shadow and a farmer's tan, he had a wide smile and something about the way he referred to my 'situation' was refreshing. He didn't swoon over it like so many of the people in town had. It was just a matter of fact to him.

I chuckled and shook his hand as I answered, "Yeah, you could say that I've had better days, but what would I know?"

Out of the corner of my eye, I saw Tandy looked mildly shocked that I'd been so jovial about the whole mess, but John let out a belly laugh and said, "They say if you've still got a sense of humor about things that it'll be alright. So Tandy says you could use some help. Walking around this town is all well and good for a stroll, but it's no way for a man to get around. I've got an extra truck just sitting around gathering rust. You can have it."

Taken aback by his kindness, I looked to Tandy for confirmation of what I'd just heard. Who offered a near total stranger a truck to use?

She smiled and nodded. "People are good in this town. We're not going to let someone literally roll into town and just flounder when we can help. That's just how it is here."

I looked back at John and said, "I can't thank you enough. That's so kind of you. But I don't have any excess cash. I'm working over at the inn for my room and board but…"

Before I could continue, John waved way my concerns. "Nah, it's no worry. I bought the thing thinking I'd fix it up, but I never did. It's run down, but it'll get you from point A to point B," he said with a shrug.

He clearly had no qualms about giving his truck away to a random stranger, and I was pretty bowled over that he'd be so nice. I shook my head and looked at both him and Tandy.

"Seriously, I can't thank you enough. When I figure out a way to repay you, I will."

The two of them just chuckled, and Tandy said, "Stop worrying so much about paying people back and worry about yourself. We can't have the local amnesia case wandering around town in the rain. It looks bad for the postcards."

"Okay. Well, I wouldn't want to mess up the postcards. Thank you, guys. Seriously."

John walked over and opened the door to his own truck. "Hop in. I'll drive you to the house and get you set up with the keys."

I threw a smile at Tandy to thank her since I had a feeling she had a big part in all of this and jumped into the truth with John. As we drove out of town and up what felt like a steep mountain and down a winding road before getting to John's place, he made pleasant small talk about how I was finding working at the inn and if I'd had the apple pie over at the Patriot. I had a feeling he wasn't just filling the time but actually cared about me, although I had no idea why. I had no sense of my past, but something inside me said I'd never met anyone as good or kind as the people in Hansonville.

We pulled up to his place and it looked exactly what you'd imagine a junk collector's yard would look like. In the middle of the property sat a small house desperately in need of a paint job by the looks of the peeling white exterior and surrounded by vehicles, parts, and pieces of random metal things that could have been from any kind of machinery. I didn't know if John had a wife or kids, but if he did, they clearly didn't spend any time outside here.

"Home sweet home. I know it probably looks terrible, but I know where each and every single thing I need here is, down to the last nut and bolt."

My eyes scanned the collection of junk in front of me. "That's saying something. You look like you've got a ton of stuff here, literally."

He shrugged at my compliment and turned off the engine. "My daddy did it before me and his before him. Guess we've got a sort of legacy going."

I nodded quietly, not knowing what else to add to his story. A blond woman in a yellow and white flowered sun dress stepped out onto the front porch ahead of us and waved. John waved back and beamed a smile.

"My wife, Shelly. I should warn you that she's going to insist you come inside and have a cup of coffee. You don't have to, but I figured you should have fair warning because it's going to happen."

Glancing over at her, I quickly decided she was out of John's league. At least looks-wise. She reminded me of one of the models in those magazines the nurses gave me to pass the time at the hospital. Her tanned arms and legs looked like she'd spent time out in the sun recently.

"I'd hate to impose, and I have to admit I've found out one thing about myself lately. More than a couple cups of coffee during the day and I'm staring at the ceiling in my room all night. Since I've already had three today, I hope your wife won't be offended."

Once again, John waved off my concerns. "Not to worry."

As he got out of the truck, I saw two children who looked like the spitting image of their mother run out to join her. Both girls, they wore their long blond hair up in ponytails that swung behind them as they talked to their mother and bounced up and down waiting for their father.

I followed behind him and heard her say, "Good afternoon. You must be the new guy in town. I'm John's wife, Shelly, and these are Sandy and Cindy."

"We're twins!" they said in unison before running around her to jump onto John.

"Would you like to have a cup of coffee?" Shelly asked after kissing her husband hello.

"Oh, I'd hate to impose," I said, unsure how

to explain that as a grown man coffee seemed to be my Kryptonite.

"I just have to find the keys to the truck. Come on in!" John said, and we all followed him through the front door.

We walked through a spotless living room and dining room back to a kitchen that looked like the exact opposite of what was going on out in the yard. Not a potholder or refrigerator magnet looked out of place, and there wasn't a single canister or appliance on the spotless counter.

I stood in the doorway while the girls and their mother focused all their attention on me and John fished through a drawer filled with keys near the sink. It felt like amongst all the pristineness and order that he'd been given a single drawer to contain his mess inside the house.

"So, how are you? Have you remembered anything about who you are yet?" Shelly asked in a sweet voice that made her question seem less rude and more curious than anything else.

Shaking my head, I answered as I did every other time I was asked that question. "Not yet. Hopefully soon."

"Do you have any big plans while you're in town?"

I hoped the answer that popped into my head wasn't obvious in my expression. Exactly what big plans anyone could have in Hansonville I had no idea. With every day I spent there, the town seemed to grow smaller and smaller.

"Not too big. I'm still getting used to the area," I lied.

Shelly nodded, and almost as if he knew he should too, John lifted his head from the drawer and did the same. I had the feeling they truly believed anyone would need more than a few hours to get their bearings in Hansonville.

"So no plans at all?" Shelly asked.

The look in her eyes said she suspected I was holding out on her, as if I'd stumbled upon some interesting part of the town no one else knew about and hadn't shared it with her. For a moment, I simply smiled, but then I wondered if she might know something about Clare that would help me.

"There's this girl…" I began to say but let my thought drift off.

She smiled broadly. "Of course, there must be a girl. A handsome young man doesn't go through life without someone. Who do you have your eye on?"

The way she said that, like I'd been out looking at used cars and finally found one that wasn't a lemon, made me chuckle. "I'm not sure I'd phrase it like that."

Shelly laughed out loud. "I like the way you put things. You better make some time to come over for dinner some night. I make a mean apple crumble."

"Well, you set the date and I'm there."

Her offer accepted, she returned to the topic I'd hoped she'd help with. "So, who is the girl?"

"Her name is Clare."

Shelly twisted her face into a quizzical expression and looked over at John. "Do I know a Clare? That name sounds familiar."

"She's the woman at the vet's office. Nice girl. Quiet."

For a moment, Shelly thought about his description of Clare, which did her little justice, and nodded. "Well, she's an odd one, they say. Keeps to herself mostly. Does she know you have your eye on her?"

Was that all anyone in this damn town could say about Clare?

"I doubt it. She doesn't seem to be interested in even making small talk with me so far," I answered truthfully.

Shelly chuckled. "Well, I'm sure she's sweet. Now John, have you found those keys? I'm sure Matt has better things to do on a hot day than hang around our house."

"Found them!" John exclaimed and then pulled out the keys to jingle them in front of his face. "Come out with me and I'll show her to you."

"It was great to meet you, Shelly."

Her blue eyes sparkled as she smiled. "It was so nice to meet you too, Matt. Remember what I said about dinner."

"I will."

Following John outside, I walked out across the yard towards the area where the truck sat. Blue with a half-worn sticker from an amusement park on the bumper, it looked a little worse for wear with a hint of rust near the front wheel. Then again, he was giving me free use of it, so who was I to notice any imperfections?

When we stopped beside it, he handed me the keys and said, "Here you go. This will make it easier to get around. And you heard the missus. She'll expect that dinner sometime soon."

"I wouldn't miss it. Just let me know. If you leave messages at the inn, I'll get them."

He smiled and patted me on the shoulder before turning to walk back into the house. Before he got too far, I yelled to him, "Hey John, one more thing before I go."

Looking back at me, he smiled. "What's that?"

"The way people talk about Clare, like there's something off about her…"

He grimaced and shook his head. "Ah, that's just small-town bullshit. I wouldn't pay any mind to it. It's just some idle nonsense for the women in town."

"From having not much else to do, I suppose," I said quietly with a shrug.

Clare didn't seem off to me. She seemed perfectly normal, other than the fact that she didn't like me.

John was probably right. Small town gossips had a way of branding people, it seemed. And they'd decided Clare was odd, and that was it.

I pushed it out of my mind and said to him, "Thanks again, man. I'll take good care of her."

"No worries. She'll do you for a while. Let me know if she starts acting up. I'll have a look under the hood if that happens."

"Will do. Tell your wife I said thank you for the offer of dinner."

With that, I got in the truck and made my best attempt not to wince when I heard the engine whine before it turned over. I looked at John and he gave me a thumbs up, a confidence I didn't share about my new ride. However, once I got going down the winding road back to town, the truck did handle nicer than I'd expected.

I was still astounded that people in Hansonville were so kind. Offering a vehicle to a random stranger wasn't what the average person did. At least I had a feeling it wasn't. It seemed I had crash-landed in a place unlike any other.

On my way into town, I passed by Clare's

house but didn't see her. I didn't care what anyone thought of her. She intrigued me, and I needed to know more about her. It was primal and pure, and I wanted to feel more of it.

I wanted her and some boring rumors about her personal life weren't going to be enough to quell my interest. I just had to figure out how to convince her of that.

CHAPTER SEVEN

Clare

AFTER A LONG day at work, I wanted nothing more than a hot shower. My muscles were so sore that I could swear the pain went deep down into my bones. I ached like I had worked hard labor despite the fact that I spent a lot of the day sitting. The animals that came in had been absolutely nuts and we all wondered if there was a full moon no one had noticed.

When I walked into the house, I ignored everything else and headed straight for my bathroom. My feet and legs ached with every step I took, and I silently prayed for sweet relief. I stood there in the shower, letting the water cascade over my body, for what seemed like hours. Scents of honey and lavender wafted around me, helping to ease the long day from my body.

Afterward, I sat down on the couch in the soft pale blue robe Emma gave me for Christmas last year. I felt the last vestiges of the day's stress slowly ebb away with each minute that passed. One of the joys of living alone in the middle of nowhere.

Grabbing my phone, I called her and waited for her to answer, sure she wasn't on shift at the hospital tonight. Maybe they were busy too, like we'd been at the vet's.

Finally, she answered, "Hey, did you change your mind and decide to come over?"

"No," I said sheepishly. "I wanted to, but I'm beat. It's was like a full moon today at work. I feel like I wrestled a herd of cattle all day. I'm sorry."

"Killjoy. But I understand. We didn't get slammed at the hospital today, thankfully, so I'm still up for doing something fun. Do you think you might get a second wind later tonight? Melissa called me today and said we could crash at her place if we wanted to drive into Philly."

The last thing I wanted to do was drive anywhere after the day I had, least of all Philly. And staying over at her cousin's apartment sleeping on the pull-out couch in her living room didn't sound appealing either.

"I don't think so. Today was a bear."

Emma chuckled. "No pun intended?"

For a few seconds, I didn't understand her joke, so she explained, "You know, because you work at a vet's?"

"Funny. No, I'm not up for anything, but

maybe tomorrow?" I offered, hating how boring I sounded.

God, I really was a killjoy!

A knock on my front door startled me out of my misery from being the dullest person around, and I sat up on my couch, immediately on guard. "Someone's at my door."

"Your door? That's strange."

"I know. Who the hell could it be?"

My shoulders tensed and I felt my jaw lock. Who would be visiting my home at seven o'clock on a Wednesday? Anxiety welled up inside me. I wasn't the type of person who got visitors, never mind at night. It was times like this that I wished I didn't live alone outside of town.

"Stay on the phone with me, okay, Emma? You know, just in case."

"Of course, but you do remember where we are, right? This is Hansonville, the safest place on the planet?"

As I walked across my living room to open the front door, I tried to remember that. Crime didn't happen around here. The last time anyone saw the inside of the Hansonville jail, it was the high school kids on a field trip last year.

Slowly, I tugged the door open and stood in shock at what I saw. Staring through the screen at me was Matt, the amnesia guy, looking as gorgeous as usual. What was he doing here?

I said nothing for a long time, and in my ear, Emma finally asked, "Who is it? Are you okay, Clare?"

"Let me call you back, okay? I might need to call the cops."

"What? Who is it? Should I jump in my car? I can be out there in three minutes if I drive fast."

Matt smiled in that sexy way I knew every woman in town loved. God, this guy had nerve!

"What are you doing here?" I asked sharply.

Before he could answer, Emma asked once more, "Who? Who's there?"

He and I silently stared each other down while I answered her. "That guy with amnesia is here. Let me call you back, but if I don't in twenty minutes, call the cops."

I ended the call as she cooed about the mysterious stranger in town. "Oooooh! I'm going to want to know every detail, Clare."

Through the screen, he chuckled. "That won't be necessary. I'm sure Sam won't appreciate having his first date with Neema ruined by some needless call to come out here."

How the hell did he know the chief of police's name and anything about his personal life? Did everyone in town just tell him everything now? He'd only been here for three weeks, for God's sake.

"What are you doing here?"

Was he some kind of creepy stalker type? I'd read horror stories about women getting stuck with guys following their every move, and I was wary of him for being at my home unannounced after following me down Main Street trying to talk to me yesterday.

He shot me one of his winning smiles and said, "I heard you lived out here and wanted to see if you needed any company."

That sounded genuine enough, but it still seemed suspicious to me.

"How did you find out where I live?" I asked, questioning him like a cop would interrogate a suspect.

My clipped tone didn't faze him, though. Still grinning, he explained, "Two women at that Patriot Restaurant mentioned that you lived out here."

It didn't sound right or true to me and even if it was true, I didn't like it. The idea of people standing around telling strangers where I lived and who knew what else about me didn't sit right. I knew people in town could be gossipy toads sometimes, but I assumed I had been largely immune recently since I never popped up on anyone's radar.

I pulled my robe closed tightly at the neck and continued questioning him. "Who? Why would two women be talking about where I live if you don't know them?"

He chuckled and stepped a little closer to the screen. "Because this is Hansonville and people around here seem more than happy to be friendly."

I didn't like his answer or the chuckle that accompanied it.

This was serious to me, so I shot back, "Then I'd guess you know lots of other people in town, so why are you here and not at their houses?"

I stepped back a little to maintain the same distance we'd had to begin with. He didn't take that hint and practically pushed his face against the screen door.

"You know, that's a nice look you have going on there with the robe. I like a woman who doesn't worry about having to wear makeup and looking picture perfect all the time."

Suddenly I remembered I wasn't at all dressed for visitors and didn't have a stitch of makeup on my face. Horrified, I shook my head in disbelief. "Oh my God! Who says something like that? You're crazy!" I said, taking another step backwards.

His face turned serious but he forced a small smile and said, "No. Just a little lonely because I don't have any memory of anything before a few weeks ago."

Damn. He sounded lost in a way I understood

all too well.

"Honestly, Clare. I'm not some weirdo stalker, if that's what you're worried about. I just wanted to see if you and I could get to know each other on a less formal basis since you shot me down about dinner."

I felt the weight of guilt settle on my shoulders. I'd been abrasive with the guy, and he didn't even know who he was. I might not be like everyone else in town, eager to embrace random strangers and tell them all my secrets, but I'd been more than aloof towards the guy. Maybe he did just want to have dinner.

With a sigh and the hope that I wouldn't end up murdered for my next decision, I shooed him away from the screen door and opened it for him. "Come in."

I tried to ensure that I sounded a little softer than before, but I didn't do a very good job of it. He smiled and stepped through the door, and I couldn't help but sense an electricity between us.

As I closed the door behind him, he looked around and asked, "So, do you live in this place all alone? It looks huge."

Brushing by his question as I started walking upstairs, I pointed toward the living room. "Just make yourself comfortable. I'll be right back."

I hurried up the stairs to my room and in a flash was out of my robe and into a blue T-shirt and jean shorts. I shook my hair out and was thankful that it fell in place nicely for once, though it was still damp. I checked myself out in the mirror and saw I looked fine, but I did wish I had been wearing makeup. I wiped under my eyes to clear the remnants of the day's mascara from beneath them and shrugged. I wasn't thrilled with how I looked, but it would be better than how he had just seen me.

I reminded myself I didn't like this guy, so I shouldn't even care what he thought about how I looked. Then again, it wasn't like he wasn't attractive. I'd be a liar if I tried to tell myself that.

The fact that he couldn't remember who he was felt like it could be an issue. That didn't have to be something dealt with tonight, though. With that in mind, I put a smile on my face and headed back downstairs to the living room.

Only to find it empty.

"Hello?" I called out, frustrated that I had to look for him in my own home.

I'd made it very clear that he was to go to the living room. I sighed and began looking around. By the time I ended up in the kitchen and saw him standing there in front of my open refrigerator, irritation coursed through me.

"Excuse me, are you always this rude when you visit people?" I asked, becoming more annoyed by the second.

He poked his head up above the door of the refrigerator and chuckled. "I have no idea. Amnesia, remember?"

His coy smile and handsome face made it hard to stay angry. Not to mention the fact that he wasn't wrong. He actually wouldn't know if he was rude in the past or not.

Still, I shut the door in front of him and said, "Is that supposed to be cute or something?"

He took a step back and smiled at me almost sadly as he replied, "Nope. Just the truth. I'm kind of going on instinct here. What about you?"

"What about me what?"

"What are you going on?" he asked as his voice dropped slightly and he took a step forward, shrinking the space between us.

Damn this man had a way about him. No wonder every woman in town seemed smitten to the point of silliness.

I glanced around the room awkwardly before looking back up at him. It was pointless to stand there and lie to myself. The guy was gorgeous. So gorgeous, in fact, that he'd been mistaken for one of the hottest movie stars in the world.

As time ticked by without me saying anything, I simply muttered, "Too much caffeine and a whole lot of sugar."

My words came out small and the stare we shared enveloped the moment. His eyes locked with mine, and I found myself unable to look away. He was handsome, and brazen, and something about him was enticing.

Even so, I backed up from him and into the living room where I felt like I wouldn't be so at the mercy of his charms. He followed, and a second later I realized I'd been wrong.

It didn't matter where I went in my own house. His effect on me unnerved me everywhere. The two of us sat down on my couch and said nothing. He didn't sit so closely that it made me uncomfortable, but he made it very clear that he had no problem being near to me.

As foolish as it may have been, I worried less about being murdered at that point, so I let myself relax a little. However, I didn't know what to say. I couldn't exactly ask him about himself. Hell, the guy didn't even know his age. It wasn't as though he could give me fun anecdotes from his life experiences or anything.

"So, have you lived here long?" he asked, suddenly seeming as awkward as me.

"All my life."

A little abrupt but the truth. This house had been in my family for years. And yet as a third generation citizen of Hansonville, I couldn't escape the feeling that I was as much a stranger in town as Matt.

"You must love it here," he said with a hint of

something I couldn't place. Disgust? Confusion?

"I bet you think the town is a little backwards. Probably not what someone like you is used to.

Matt shrugged and shook his head. "Again, amnesia. I don't know what I'm used to."

Jesus, this was more difficult than any conversation I'd ever had with a man, and I didn't have a long history of success with the opposite sex. Surprising how dependent on the past someone had to be to get through a basic conversation.

"Oh. Yeah. I'm sorry. You'd think I'd be able to remember that."

My apology brought a smile to his face that I had to admit made him even more attractive than before. "That makes two of us not able to remember," he said with a chuckle.

Unsure what to say to that, I fell back on what I knew all too well. Pushing people away. Standing, I announced, "I'm glad you stopped by, but I do need to get going to bed."

He seemed surprised, and his eyebrows shot up into his forehead as he glanced at the old cuckoo clock before looking back at me. "It's not even nine o'clock yet."

"Yes. Well, some of us like to sleep after a long day at work, you know."

My answer appeared to satisfy him, although he didn't stand to leave like he should have.

"Is it that you just don't like me? Like you couldn't say you had to wash your hair, so you went for the second-best excuse, going to bed early?"

I was taken aback by the abruptness of his statement. He was so blunt and forward that it was disarming to say the very least. I stammered out what amounted to nothing for a few seconds before finally saying clearly, "I don't not like you."

"Well, that's a ringing endorsement if I've ever heard one."

The crestfallen look on his face signaled that what I said disappointed him. I felt bad for making someone who was clearly trying his hardest feel bad. Damn. Maybe I was that odd bird everyone said I was.

"What about this? We can do this again tomorrow night, and if you still can't say anything better about me than you don't not like me, I'll go away and never bother you again."

I let out a small sigh of frustration and started to say something about how we shouldn't be starting anything, especially with his mind in the state it was in. Before I could manage to get out a full sentence, though, Matt stood and closed the space between us before pressing his lips to mine.

It felt like a jolt of electricity flew from his lips to mine and down to the deepest parts of me. My knees nearly buckled as I stood there motionless. His kiss was deep but not invasive. He held me gently at the waist, and it felt warm and safe. Just as I was starting to fully get lost in his kiss, he pulled back, leaving me standing there with my eyes closed and my head still tilted up.

I corrected myself after a second and felt a blush rising into my cheeks as I simply said, "Okay." I wished I had more to say, but nothing came out.

"Great! It's a date. Say six?"

My head swam with the sensation of that incredible kiss as I nodded. "Six sounds good."

Giving me a wink, Matt smiled. "I promise you won't regret it, Clare."

As I stood there in semi-shock at how easily I'd allowed myself to be lured in by him, he let himself out, leaving me wondering if I'd made a terrible mistake. Not that the kiss hadn't been amazing. God, I needed a better word than amazing for how great he kissed.

But that didn't change the fact that I had no idea who he truly was just as he didn't. Maybe he hadn't been a serial killer in his previous life, but that didn't mean he was a good man either. While the tragic irony of the town outcast being courted by the town amnesiac couldn't be ignored, it didn't obscure the truth of my romantic history.

Things with men and me didn't work out.

They just didn't. Over and over, I'd wasted a ton of time and energy and what did it ever amount to? Nothing.

But as I turned off all the lights and slowly made my way up to my bed, I wondered to myself if it was time I let myself enjoy a little company. Was it so wrong for me to think that a gorgeous man interested in me could be a good thing? I didn't imagine it would work out long term, nothing ever did, but I could still have a little fun.

I just couldn't get too close.

Yes, that would have to be the compromise I made with myself. I couldn't get too close. I couldn't get my hopes up. I could only have a little fun and not hurt him or let myself get hurt by getting too close.

Laying my head down onto the pillow, I closed my eyes and replayed that kiss with Matt. So maybe he was a man with no memory of the past and I was a woman who couldn't think of anything but the past. That didn't mean we were doomed, right?

I simply wouldn't get too close. I couldn't.

CHAPTER EIGHT

Matt

I WALKED AWAY from Clare's front porch wearing a huge grin of satisfaction. She might act as if she didn't like me, but I could tell from that kiss that she was interested.

Interested might even have been putting it lightly. I had a feeling she wanted me about as much as I wanted her.

Physically, at least, and there was not a damn thing wrong with that, in my opinion. We were just seeing where this could go. No problem with that.

I hopped into the truck John had set me up with, and about a mile and a half down the road felt like I finally exhaled. I liked Clare. I liked her a lot. Since the first time we met at the hospital, I couldn't stop thinking about her. I had no way of knowing if that had ever happened to me before, but I knew what I felt for her was real.

The idea that I had a wife or someone waiting

for me somewhere in the world did occur to me, but at the moment in the middle of nowhere, I didn't care. I would deal with all of that when it came time. If I was stuck not remembering anything from my real life, then I would fill my new memories up with the beautiful and aloof woman I was obviously falling for. Something about the way she wanted me to think she didn't care at all when all it took was one kiss to know the truth existed somewhere far different enchanted me, and I wanted to know more.

She'd agreed to give me a shot, so I needed to make sure I didn't waste it. I didn't plan on merely showing her I was a great guy. I wanted to full on woo her.

And that meant I needed to pull out all the stops. Well, at least all the stops I could pull out in a small town like Hansonville and on the tiny amount of money I'd saved up in my time working for Sarah at the Colonial Inn.

I pulled into the empty grocery store parking lot to think about how I wanted to go about things. I had no idea what she liked other than living in a big house alone and animals. She worked for a vet's office, that much I knew, so she clearly couldn't hate animals.

Damnit. That meant nothing. What could I talk to her about other than animals? I had no past, and she didn't exactly give up a lot about herself. This date would run about ten minutes before she walked away and never spoke to me again.

As I racked my brain, I looked out of the front windshield and saw two women happily chatting away as they walked out of the now-closed grocery store. That's when it hit me. If I was going to figure out how to seduce Clare, I needed to talk to someone who really knew her.

Her friend from the hospital, Emma.

Lucky for me, I knew exactly where to find her. I put the truck in gear and headed back to the inn to sleep. As far as I knew, Emma worked days so I'd visit her in the morning.

WHEN I DROVE up to the hospital, I got a few stares from the locals but nothing nearly as bad as the first time I'd been there. Then I'd felt like some kind of animal in a zoo.

Now everyone just smiled and nodded at me as I walked in. Just inside the doors, I passed one woman who looked me up and down and whispered to the man next to her, "That Matt really has fit in here, hasn't he?"

Maybe she meant she liked the way my T-shirt fit.

It only took a few minutes of wandering around the halls to find Emma. I spied her writing something down on a clipboard at the second floor nurses' station.

"Emma, hey, how are you?" I said, wishing I had a better lead in prepared.

She raised her eyebrows in surprise, but when her eyes settled on my face, she smiled. "Good morning, Matt. How are you today?"

I had a feeling she may have liked me more than I liked her, so I was careful to get right to the point. I didn't need that kind of confusion muddying up what I wanted to do with Clare.

"I'm good, Emma. I wanted to talk to you about something. Do you have a few minutes?"

Her smile didn't fade as she nodded slightly. "Well, I'm about to take a break, so we can go to the cafeteria if you want."

"You weren't planning on going to lunch with Clare, were you?"

She shook her head. "No. She's tied up with work today. Come on, we can go chat in the cafeteria."

We sat down after she'd gotten her food and scowled at me as I sat with nothing in front of me. "Are you eating? It's not just your mind that needs to get healthy, you know. You weren't busted up too badly, but you must've taken some kind of spill to lose your memory."

She paused and let out a sigh. "Okay, that's all I have for my nurse's speech, so now I'll return to my regular friendly neighborhood Emma."

I chuckled at her attempt to lecture me. "No worries. I had a big breakfast."

"You better have. Now what is it you wanted to talk about?" she asked with a knowing look.

I launched into my idea, jumping in with both feet. "I like Clare. I've tried connecting with her, but I haven't had much success. Everyone else in this town seems to welcome me with open arms, but I can't seem to make much headway with her."

Emma smiled. "Clare isn't the kind of woman who gives off neon signs about how she feels."

Rolling my eyes at that little nugget of truth, I continued. "Tell me about it. I did get her to agree to see me this evening. I don't know why, but she seems hesitant to start something with me. I know the amnesia thing gets in the way, but I've told her I don't care so she shouldn't either."

"Spoken like a typical man," Emma said, twisting her face into a smirk.

"She likes me. I know she does. She isn't exactly falling over herself to be with me, though. I'm not an idiot. I get dating an amnesiac comes with some issues, but when I figure out my past, I'm not just going to bail on her. I don't love anyone. I can feel that. I know it sounds crazy, but I can just tell."

With a sweet smile, she shook her head. "Well, first of all, you don't sound crazy. You sound sincere. I can't speak to your situation much, though. Amnesia is tricky, and each case is different. Some people regain their memories in hours, and some never do. That's much rarer but always a possibility. I don't mean to be a huge bummer. I'm sure you'll remember everything soon. But to be honest, when it comes to my best friend, the amnesia part might not even be the biggest obstacle."

That didn't sound good. "What do you mean?"

Emma sighed. "Clare has a way of pushing every man away. It isn't your fault. Hell, it's not even Clare's fault entirely. She's just seriously gun shy when it comes to anything even remotely resembling romance. It goes back to her being a kid."

I looked at her in confusion. What did Clare's childhood have to do with this?

"You really want to hear this? I won't lie. It doesn't foretell great things for you."

Without hesitation, I nodded. "Yes, I do. I like her, and I want to understand."

Again, Emma sighed, this time deeper. "We met when we were young, and from a kid's point of view, her family was great. Clare's an only child, but when she was seven, her mother miscarried. I don't think she ever recovered, to be honest. From that day on, it was like some kind of cloud came over their house. Nothing seemed the same. Her mother sometimes didn't leave the bedroom for days. Clare didn't understand what was happening, and I don't think her father did either. When she was about nine, her mother left. One day, she was just gone. Her father was heartbroken, but Clare hadn't just lost her mother. She'd lost one of the people she'd been taught to trust."

"Damn. That's awful. Did she ever see her mother again?"

I couldn't imagine what it must have been like to have been abandoned at such a young age by her mother. I knew from Emma's face and tone though that this wasn't going to be some fairy-tale ending for Clare and her parents. It hurt my heart already to know that something like that had happened to her.

"She did, and like a cruel joke from the universe, it made it worse. Her mother had met a guy that got her hooked on the hard stuff. When Clare turned eighteen, she found her dying from the drugs. The guy had left her years before, so she had no one. It's like Clare had something good dangled in front of her only to have it yanked away soon after."

Now it was my turn to sigh. Nothing I'd imagined about Clare had been this bad. "She still had her father, right?"

Emma nodded sadly. "Yeah. He adored Clare. Never remarried. Hell, he never even dated as far as anyone knew, and everyone knows everything in this town. He was a nice guy and he wasn't ugly or anything. He was just heartbroken. He even tolerated us having loud giggle sleepovers when we were younger. I think he wanted Clare to have friends because somehow the love of a friend was safe. Love from romantic partners, however, no way."

"Okay, so her parents didn't exactly give her a good model of love. That doesn't mean she has to believe it can't happen to her."

I could see how that might make someone a little apprehensive about maybe jumping into marriage, but it seemed silly that it would prevent them wanting to date at all. I felt like I wasn't getting the full story.

"No. At least not in the romantic sense. Clare's father adored her, though. She was his whole world, especially after her mother left. He was obviously lonely. You could see it in his face anytime he talked to you. It was like losing his wife hollowed him out. But he and Clare had a very close relationship, and when he died, she was devastated."

"Well, I'll just have to show her that I'm not like her mother, Emma. She'll see that, and it's not like I'm expecting her to settle down and move in with me."

Standing from the table, I smiled down at her. "Thanks for the heads up. I appreciate it."

Emma grabbed my arm to stop me as I turned to leave. I looked down and saw by her sad expression that she had more to tell me.

"Hang on. That's not the worst of it."

Having her mother abandon her and seeing her father brokenhearted every day until he died wasn't the worst of it? Jesus. What else could there be?

As I sat back down, I wished the hospital cafeteria served liquor. I had a feeling I'd need a drink after this.

"When Clare was twenty-two, she fell in love with the new guy in Hansonville. You've seen how we treat newcomers here. The whole town loved Colin. But no one loved him more than Clare. They were crazy about one another. Their romance was one for the ages. It started hot and heavy and took her breath away. He wooed her like crazy and was nicer to her than any guy in the world had been before, not that she's seen much of it. It wasn't long before everyone was hearing wedding bells for them."

"I have a feeling I know where this is going." I said, feeling worse for Clare by the second.

"Yup. They were all set to be married. I'd never seen her happier. He'd proposed to her outside of the Patriot where they'd gone on their first date. It was more of a public spectacle than I think she would have preferred, but for once she didn't care if the whole town looked at her. She was happy. We spent our lunches talking about bridesmaid dresses and color schemes. She was in heaven. We all figured that she'd had some bad luck earlier in life because of her mother, but lots of people do. Then one day this guy comes to her and says he can't marry her. He never explained why. The next day he left town and we've never heard from him again."

I sat there stunned, my chest tight from this story. "Are you kidding me? Wow. That's messed up. All of this is messed up."

"Yeah, it is," Emma said before taking a bite of her sandwich. "That was six years ago, and she's never really gotten over it. Ever since then, if any guy gets too close, she just ends it and leaves them heartbroken and coming to me asking why. You're one step ahead, though. You came to me first."

"Damn. That's a lot for one person to deal with. But I'm not those other guys. I'm not going to let that happen."

"I wish I could say things will be different this time, but history isn't on your side, Matt. Sorry."

But I wasn't giving up that easily. "I want to know what she likes. What makes her happy? I don't want to mess this up. I know she thinks I just want to get in her pants, but that's not what I'm doing. Tell me something that can help me show her that, will you?"

Emma looked at me skeptically. I sensed she was weighing her choices. "I don't know, Matt. I mean…"

"I'm not asking for her social security number. I just want to know some stuff she likes so I can make a good impression and show her that I like her enough to do that."

"Fine. But I'm not giving you any creepy personal details. Don't be weird. But I'll let you know some of the more innocent and benign stuff, I guess."

"Fine. That's all I ask."

"She has this thing with penguins."

"Penguins?"

Was I expected to show up at this woman's house with a penguin? I didn't know much about this part of Pennsylvania, but I was fairly sure this wasn't where penguins hung out.

"Yeah, penguins. She loves them. No idea why. She just does. I guess they're kind of cute the way they waddle around. Oh, and macaroni and cheese. I'm not talking about the homemade kind. That stuff is at least sometimes tolerable. She likes the box kind from the grocery store. I find it disgusting. But hey, it's her food. If she likes it, so be it," she said with a shrug.

"Penguins and macaroni and cheese," I repeated, wondering what I could do to incorporate both of those.

"I hate macaroni and cheese. You couldn't pay me enough to eat it," I said with a chuckle.

Just the idea of wet milky cheese product sliding around noodles was enough to make my stomach turn. Disgusting.

"I agree. It's what she likes, though. Oh, and of course, bluegrass music. But that I can see why. It's good music. We've been to a few bluegrass shows together, and she loves it."

I sighed. "So, penguins, macaroni and cheese, and bluegrass music is what I have to work with. How is any of that going to help me by tonight when we have our first official date?"

Emma thought for a moment, staring down at the table as she ate, before lifting her head and smiling. "Oh, I've got it! You can get a stuffed penguin from Clark's Gift Store. It's a few doors down from the Patriot Restaurant. You can't miss it. Since you hate macaroni and cheese, that one is out. But how about I grab you a couple of my bluegrass CDs that I can lend you. I know she'd love them. You could throw the CD on in that truck I hear you've got now and take a nice drive with her. That could be really romantic."

My hope quickly turned to disappointment.

"Only one problem with that. The truck doesn't have a CD player."

Emma's shoulders sagged like the news about my truck defeated her. "Damn."

We both sat in silence as no ideas seemed to be coming. Before we could brainstorm any more, a female's voice came over the loudspeaker to call Emma back to work.

She gave me a tiny smile before standing from the table to leave. "Let me know if you need the CDs. I hope it goes well for you, Matt. You seem really nice."

"Thank for all your help, Emma."

She gathered up the remains of her lunch and disappeared in a flash, leaving me to figure out what to do on my date tonight. How in the world was I supposed to conjure up some kind of magic involving penguins, of all things? Why couldn't she like puppies?

I sighed and began to feel as defeated as Emma had looked. Clare worked at a vet's office, so no wonder she liked such a foreign animal. She'd probably never gotten to see one in person. Still, what was I supposed to do with that?

I walked outside into the warm summer sun and sat down on a bench near the entrance of the hospital to think things over. Emma had mentioned something about a stuffed penguin. That might work, but it felt lame. Maybe inside the penguin could be macaroni and cheese?

Jesus, no. That sounded utterly revolting.

But before I could get too caught up in that disgusting thought, I realized that I might just have an idea for our date after all. I rushed to the truck to set my plan in action.

CHAPTER NINE

Clare

"THIS ISN'T GOING to work. They never work out," I muttered to myself as I got ready in my bedroom for my night with Matt.

Men and I never worked out.

My apprehension wasn't nerves about going out with a hot guy like Matt. Well, maybe a little about that. Hansonville had its share of bachelors, but most of them tended to be young kids fresh out of high school. Some of them were really good looking, but at twenty-eight, it felt downright creepy to be checking them out.

Not that Emma and I didn't sneak a look every once in a while. We were mature adults, but we weren't dead.

I'd picked the pink sundress that brought out the blue in my eyes and made me feel beautiful. I still had the remnants of a tan from the four visits to the salon a month ago with Emma, so I looked sun kissed. My hair had chosen to behave, which was always a welcome surprise, and my makeup went on perfectly, so I should have felt great.

But still I doubted any of this was worth the effort. I stared down blankly at my sunflower bedspread as my mind drifted back to that night when Colin told me the wedding couldn't happen. My chest tightened like someone held me in a vice, and getting a full breath of air into my lungs became impossible.

Don't do this, Clare. You always do this. Every damn time you do this. Just fucking stop. Colin was one man. So it didn't work. Don't let that ruin the rest of your life.

One man who I thought would help me break the curse of my family's unhappiness and who I'd get a happily ever after with. One man I loved.

The man I thought loved me.

I shook my head to dispel the negative thoughts back to their usual hiding places in the back of my mind. I couldn't let myself become like my father. He never gave anyone a chance after my mother left and died lonely, even if he did have me.

That didn't have to be my fate, though. I just needed to give people a chance. Or at least that's what Emma had told me until she practically turned blue in the face.

So tonight I wanted to do that. Give someone a chance.

I spritzed some perfume onto my neck and wrists and took one final look at myself in the mirror. Emma always said you can tell when a person wears a cloak of insecurity. Even though it was invisible, you can always see it.

Whenever those words came out of her mouth, I wondered who used the word cloak anymore, needing to dismiss her claim since I knew she meant me too, even if the comment was directed at someone else. Scanning my reflection, I smiled and silently hoped that would help me shed my own cloak.

And a second later, it came raging back with a thousand possibilities how this night could go wrong. With my luck, he was going to figure out who he was halfway through dinner and remember he had a wife, and kids, maybe a dog, a gerbil, who knew? As much as he seemed fine with glossing over that huge detail, clearly I couldn't.

Last night, I'd made sure to sneak a glance more than once to see if I could find any hint of a wedding ring line on his ring finger. I didn't see one. But that didn't mean anything. More than a few married men didn't wear wedding bands.

Or maybe he had a girlfriend or fiancé. No one that good looking was single. It was just a law of the universe.

I let out a large sigh and flopped down onto

my bed. Why couldn't I just be like other women? Emma, for example, never failed to get excited about seeing someone new. Every new man for her was a potential husband, and she dove in head first to see if that was actually the case.

Not me. I did this every single time. I wanted so badly to just be filled with butterflies from excitement instead of from apprehension and dread. I wanted to feel that electricity course through my body instead of feeling like at any moment I might throw up.

It wasn't healthy, but it was who I'd been for so long. Every time a man showed any interest in me, my mind automatically jumped to all the worst-case scenarios it could concoct. I wanted to enjoy my time with a man instead of trying to chase them away.

If it never went too far, I couldn't get that hurt in the long run, so the tradeoff seemed okay. That's what I'd already decided would have to happen with Matt. I wasn't going to get overly attached to a man whose name neither of us actually knew and whose real life was a complete mystery to everyone, including him.

But maybe this time I could just let go of the pain and enjoy myself? It couldn't hurt to have a few smiles and laugh with someone I liked. Could it?

I sat up and caught my reflection in the

mirror. I looked terrified. I wanted to give him a chance, I wanted to give love a chance in general, but then the painful memory of what my mother did to my father came rushing back. I may have been young, but kids pick up on more than adults give them credit for. Plus, it's not as though my father had been secretive about his feelings on the matter. Overnight he went from a stoic but happy and affectionate man to a bitter one who resented someone so much that it consumed him. I grew up hearing the same thing from him over and over.

"Love brings you nothing but heartache, Clare. My only wish for you is that you never have to go through that pain."

He never knew this, but it hurt me to hear the sadness behind those words my whole life.

And then I got my own real life lesson in just how right he was.

As I stood up and walked away from the mirror, I wondered if maybe it was best to just forget about love. It was the twenty-first century, even if much of Hansonville didn't seem to know that yet. Two people could have a good time without ending up married with two kids, a mortgage, and plans for the rest of their lives.

Maybe I could convince myself that settling for a good time would be enough.

I heard a knock on the front door and took a

deep breath in. I could do this. It was just a date. Nothing big. Nobody got hurt from a single date, right?

One date.

My heart racing, I hurried down to answer the door. Standing on the porch, Matt smiled, and I scanned his body from head to toe in surprise to see him wearing a blue dress shirt and black pants. He looked fantastic.

"Wow. You look great, Matt," I said with a smile, momentarily a bit stunned. But how could he have afforded the new shirt and pants?

Suspicious, I asked him, "How did you manage to get these clothes?"

He looked down his body and then back up at me. "I may have spent all the money I had on them. Since I'm working at the hotel, I've got some money coming in, so it's all good," he answered with a deep chuckle.

That he'd made that effort to impress me made me smile. He didn't have to do that. Then just as I noticed he had his hand hidden behind his back, he pulled it forward and held a stuffed penguin out in front of him.

"I happened to see this while walking past the card store in town and thought you might like it."

My mouth dropped open. A penguin stuffed animal? Did he know that was my favorite animal?

No. He couldn't. Impossible. Penguins had become more popular recently, so it certainly had to be a coincidence.

Still, I couldn't help but be charmed by his gift. I smiled and opened the screen door to take the penguin in my hand. "That's so nice. Thank you."

"His name is Petey the Penguin. Watch him. He's got a way about him I hear that makes it easy to fall in love with him."

I looked up from the stuffed animal and smiled. "Petey the Penguin, huh?"

"So I hear."

"Thank you so much. You didn't have to do this."

"Well, I may not have any memory of my past, but I watch enough TV at night to know showing up for a date empty-handed is a definite no. Or maybe that's just on the Hallmark Channel, which seems to be the single channel that works on the TV in my room."

I couldn't help but laugh as I thought of a grown man spending night after night with the Hallmark Channel and its oh-so-sweet and romantic shows. "You poor man. That must be like hell for you," I joked.

Matt shrugged. "It was at first, but I have to admit you sort of get used to it. I think there's some brainwashing going on there, but it's all I have for the time being."

"Come on in," I offered, holding the screen door open for him.

We walked over to my couch and sat down together with Petey the Penguin on my lap. Staring straight ahead, I tried to think of something to say, but I drew a blank. Matt appeared to have the same problem since we just sat there in awkward silence.

Finally, he cleared his throat and said, "You look beautiful, by the way. Sorry. I forgot to say that. Forgetting is kind of my thing, you see."

I looked over at him and chuckled. He really liked using the amnesiac thing to his benefit. I supposed I couldn't blame him. I probably would have too.

"Thank you. That's sweet of you to say."

I knew I wasn't offering much in the way of conversation, but I genuinely didn't know what to say. I never did. It wasn't that I was some socially awkward creature. Most of the time, I just didn't like speaking for the sake of filling up the silence. I spoke when I had something to say and sometimes I just didn't.

However, at this moment, I didn't know what to say, suddenly.

After a few more moments of silence, Matt cleared his throat again and said, "Well, if you're ready, we have to leave soon."

"We do?" I asked, surprised we had an actual schedule. I'd assumed we'd get dinner somewhere, but since the Patriot was open for a few hours more and finding an empty table at this time of night wasn't exactly a challenge, what was his hurry?

With a broad smile that lit up his dark eyes, he nodded. "Yes. We've got plans tonight."

"Where are we going?" I asked.

Weekdays in Hansonville meant exactly nothing would be happening. Hell, even the weekends weren't jam packed with excitement in my tiny town. Sometimes there was a farmer's market on Saturday mornings. That was nice when they had peaches to sell. But in a town with two bars, one of which was a VFW, the town wasn't exactly fun central.

Matt stood up and held out his hand for me to take. "I can't tell you. It's a surprise. But we really do have to go or we won't make it on time."

For a moment, I considered protesting because he wouldn't give me the details about our date, but I sort of liked the idea of him taking control of this. Most of all, I wanted to go since I rarely left the house other than to go to work or hang out with Emma.

I just wasn't thrilled not knowing where I was being taken with a strange man. I made a mental note to shoot Emma a text when we got on the road and then again wherever we ended up, just in case.

"Okay. Let me grab my purse."

I locked up behind us and followed him to the truck. A perfect gentleman, he opened my door for me, offering his hand as I stepped up into the truck.

He got in on his side and I said, "I'd heard around town that someone had given you a truck. I'm glad you're not stuck wandering the streets."

He nodded and I could tell he was a little embarrassed when he replied, "I know it's a bit of an eyesore, but John was nice enough to give it to me and even if it's ugly, it's a blessing."

"Oh, it's totally fine! If it gets you from point A to point B, that's all that matters. Plus, we both know your situation is…"

I stopped talking, unsure how to describe all he'd been through. I didn't want to insult him. What did you call not knowing your past and being forced to make your way nearly blindly in a strange place?

He chuckled and finished my sentence for me. "Unique?"

I liked that better than anything that popped into my mind. "Yes, I think unique would be a good word for it."

He put the truck in gear and flashed me a sexy smile that made my stomach do a flip. So much for wanting to push him away. My brain may have thought that would be the plan, but clearly the rest of me had other ideas.

Sexier ideas.

Okay, Clare. Slow down. Yes, he looks incredible in that shirt that fits perfectly over his muscular chest. And yes, that one glance you took at his ass in those dress pants certainly wasn't bad. But that doesn't mean anything.

Even though I couldn't deny I wouldn't mind it meaning something.

As we rode along, I had to admit to being quietly impressed with how everyone in town seemed to like him so much. People from Hansonville, while sometimes puritanical and gossipy, were good and decent-hearted people deep down, but I hadn't heard of them just giving random strangers a place to stay and a truck. He really must have made an impression on people.

Either that or they couldn't say no to a handsome face. I could hardly blame them. The guy was stunning.

"People must have really taken to you if they're loaning you their truck. They must like you."

Although I'd meant it as a compliment, he looked a little down when he responded, "Nah. They pity me because I'm that guy in Hansonville with no memory. That's how they refer to me around town when I hear them whispering and they don't think I can hear them. Not that them calling me Matt is much different. I'm feeling pretty sure it's not my name."

"Well, I don't think you're just the guy with no memory," I offered, knowing it wouldn't do anything to make him feel much better.

Hoping to change the subject but not too obviously, I quickly followed up with, "Did you find that you had to remember how to drive?"

He glanced over at me as we went around a turn in the road. "No, but that's because the doctor says it's muscle memory and that's different from the memory that the amnesia affects. I could probably still ride a bike, he says, not that I've tried."

The truck picked up speed after he shifted into third gear, and we began to cruise down the highway. I noticed we were headed east out of Hansonville, but I swallowed the question about where we were going.

Instead, I said, "I haven't ridden a bike in so long. Maybe this summer I'll do that. When I was little my bike might as well have been attached to me surgically. You couldn't get me off the thing."

As soon as the words left my mouth, I sat there in the passenger seat surprised at myself. I usually didn't offer details like that to people so quickly. Out of everyone in town, only Emma really knew anything real about me. We'd been friends since she'd moved to town in second grade, so of course, she knew everything about me.

When Matt didn't say anything to my odd confession about my childhood, I grew uncomfortable and joked, "Okay Rico Suave, where are we going? You've got to tell me."

He grinned and replied, "You already know my answer to that. By the way, who is Rico Suave?"

I threw my head back and laughed at his question, which bordered on ridiculous. "Sorry. If you don't remember your name, you certainly wouldn't remember that name from some obscure eighties song the local radio station seems to love to play lately."

Matt looked over at me with confusion. "Eighties? I can't remember just over a month ago. Decades are definitely out of the question."

"Well, forget that. Just tell me where we're going."

He simply shook his head. "Nope."

"Let me guess," I said. "You can't tell me because if you did, then it wouldn't be a surprise anymore, right?"

"Exactly. But I promise you're going to enjoy it."

"I don't know how you can be so sure about

that, but I guess I have to give you the benefit of the doubt." He had no idea how hard that was for me.

Looking over at me, he flashed me that winning grin of his and said, "Yes. I'll be using that to my advantage, by the way."

I laughed at his boldness. "I think that's fine for now, but you should know I can only keep my curiosity at bay for a short time."

We settled into a conversation about my work and talked about the small towns we were passing with their silly billboards about random attractions they offered. The inn that claimed to have the fork George Washington once used. The cemetery that supposedly held the grave of some famous Civil War general. The store that proudly claimed to sell items William Penn's family owned. Typical small-town gimmicks I was used to since I'd seen them all my life but I imagined seemed utterly odd to someone like Matt.

The time passed quickly, and while I still wasn't sure where we were headed, after about an hour on the road, I found I didn't mind so much.

CHAPTER TEN

Matt

T HE DRIVE TOOK nearly an hour and a half, but it flew by in a snap because Clare and I talked like we had known each other for a lifetime. After what Emma told me, I'd expected her to be closed off and I'd have to coax her out of her shell, but something seemed different about her tonight. Gone was the aloof woman, replaced by one who acted like she wanted to give me a chance.

I planned on taking advantage of that opportunity so tonight wouldn't be our only date.

I didn't know what to expect of the place I was taking her, a bar called Jasper's, but as I drove into the dirt parking lot, I didn't think it looked too bad. In front of me stood a small, concrete building with a red awning above the front door and a wooden patio off the side. A group of people gathered outside to smoke while music flowed from inside the bar, the signature sounds of a fiddle and banjo filling the air.

Clare clamped her hand onto my forearm and squealed, "Oh my God! You brought me to a bluegrass show? I can't believe it! How did you know I love bluegrass?"

I loved how excited my surprise made her, but I wanted to give Emma her due. "I must confess. I stopped by the hospital and asked your friend. She told me you loved this kind of music, so I looked into where we could hear some tonight. This is supposed to be a good place for it."

She shook her head and smiled. "This is so cool of you, Matt."

"I didn't want to blow my chance by taking you to the VFW," I admitted with a chuckle.

That definitely wouldn't have helped me make a good impression.

She laughed and nodded, "Well, big points for not taking me to Hansonville's official old man bar, for sure. I can't wait to get in here and hear some music. Let's go!"

Grabbing my hand, she pulled me toward the front door. I looked at her, truly shocked at how open she was now. It was like a complete change in her personality. We walked in and I bought us both drinks at the bar before we found a table close enough to the small bandstand for us to hear the band and one another. For a few songs, she sipped her drink and listened to the band quietly, but I saw her foot and finger tapping and knew she was into it.

"Have you been to this place before?" I asked between songs.

She shook her head. "No, but if they have live bluegrass all the time like this, I might just have to come back. It's a nice place."

I looked around and thought to myself that nice wouldn't be the way I'd describe Jasper's. Rundown fit better. Maybe calling it a hole-in-the-wall would be right.

"You don't like this place, do you?" she asked, leaning over toward me as the music began again.

"To be honest, I don't know. I can't say I feel right at home here, but it's not too bad."

Clare smiled and shook her head. "I wouldn't care if it was a dive. I love the music. And I suppose the company isn't too bad."

She was toying with me, but I didn't mind. I liked this version of her much more compared to the closed off version.

"I agree. The company is pretty good," I said with a smile.

A second later, she held out her hand in front of me. "You have to dance. You know that, right?"

"Have to?" I asked as I looked down at her hand in horror.

I had no idea if I danced, well or not, but I

had a real suspicion I didn't dance to bluegrass.

"You aren't going to tell me you don't dance, are you?" she asked with a sexy smile and sparkle in her eye.

"I have no memory of ever dancing," I said honestly.

"Come on. It'll be great!"

I placed my hand in hers and shook my head. "I don't know. This might end badly."

"Don't think like that. We don't know a soul here. Even if we're terrible, it won't matter."

We walked hand in hand to the dance floor filled mostly with people who looked like they were at least sixty years old. But damn those old people could move. I watched in awe as their legs rapidly shot out to the front and the side like they were made of elastic.

I leaned in toward Clare and said in her ear, "I can't dance like this! I don't even know what they're doing."

She laughed and pointed toward their feet. "It's called clogging, but we don't have do those steps. Just follow me and we'll be fine."

A couple nearby smiled at us as I stood amazed at how spry these people around us were. I had a feeling I might break one of my legs if I tried to do these steps.

"You ready?" she asked in my ear as the music began to pick up.

A single word filled my head. No. But I didn't want to ruin our date now that Clare had actually blossomed into this incredible woman even I hadn't imagined she had inside her, so I plastered a smile on my face and hoped I didn't make a complete ass of myself in a few seconds.

She took my hand like we were going to slow dance and nodded. "All we have to do is move to the music. Just follow me, okay?"

We started to dance, and to my surprise, she was really great at it. The way she moved her body to the beat mesmerized me. As I suspected, I danced like a one-legged drunk man, so I just let her do her thing and tried my best to keep up.

When the song died down and the next one picked up a few seconds later, she didn't seem to have any interest in going back to the table and instead kept right at it. After two more songs, I needed a break, and as if the band could tell, they switched to a slow song next. Clare smiled shyly, and I took her hand in mine. This kind of dancing I could do.

Pulling her close to me, I took a deep breath in at the feel of her body next to mine. She smelled like honey and flowers.

"I promise I'm better at this kind of dancing," I said as we swayed back and forth to the music.

She blushed as she replied, "I didn't think you were bad at the other kind. It just takes a little getting used to."

"Thanks. I'm not sure how good I was, but I like this better."

The music seemed to fade away, along with all the people around us, until it was just Clare and me. I'd waited for this moment since the first time I met her and swore I'd get her to give me a chance. Now that I had it, I didn't want to mess it up.

She looked up at me with those soft blue eyes of hers, and in them I thought I saw a hint of something that said she wasn't sure about me. As much as I wanted to kiss her right there, I didn't. Better to not push and ruin any chances for what I hoped we'd get to later.

As if she sensed my deliberations, she said, "You got quiet there. Is anything wrong?"

"Well, I'm not sure dancing is one of my skills, to be honest. I imagine there's some girl who attended prom with me somewhere still nursing sore feet. I guess I didn't think this date all the way through when I decided to bring you here, but I'm glad you came out with me tonight, Clare."

"Me too."

She leaned her head against my chest, and together, we gently rocked back and forth to the music like we were the only two people in that bar. One of the older guys gave me a thumbs up and a wink, and his wife nodded. Well, at least I had the approval of those two cloggers for what I hoped was happening between Clare and me.

I smiled back and closed my eyes to enjoy the sweet smell of Clare's hair gently wafting up from below. She was warm against me, and her breasts gently rose and fell against my chest as she breathed. It was one of the best moments I'd enjoyed since that day I woke up on the side of Highway 27.

I PULLED INTO Clare's driveway and turned off the truck. Of course, it had to do that backfire thing it liked to do to kill the mood. Not that I had a sense exactly what kind of mood Clare and I had going at that point. We'd had a great time at the bar, but the ride home had been quiet.

Too quiet.

Sitting there in the dark, I tried to decide if I should just make my move or try some more conversation. As that tug of war went on inside my head, I knew I should just bite the bullet and kiss her. I'd been dying to for hours, so why not?

"Is something wrong, Matt?" I heard her ask, instantly pulling me out of my indecisive thoughts.

I turned in my seat and looked over toward

her in the pitch blackness. The quarter moon did little to help me see her expression, but I knew by the tone of her voice that she wondered what the hell was wrong with me.

She wasn't alone. I couldn't figure out what the problem was either.

Maybe I'd always been a jackass when it came to women. I didn't want to think of myself as a total loser with the opposite sex, but at least that would explain me not doing what any red-blooded American male should want to do with Clare at that moment.

I'd thought about this nearly every night for the past few weeks. Hell, I'd more than thought of it. That healthy American male side of me didn't seem to have any issues with fantasizing about her each night in my room at the Colonial Inn.

So what the fuck was going on with me now?

Before I could answer her question, she mumbled something about needing to get inside and jumped out of the truck. I watched the outline of her run up to her house, as if she needed to escape from me and all my idiocy.

You're blowing it, man! Get out of this goddamned truck and chase after her!

My fingers fumbled around the steering column trying to find the keys, wasting more precious time, but then I found them and hurriedly yanked them out of the ignition. By the time I got out of the truck, Clare had shut the front door and turned the hallway light on to go upstairs.

I needed to catch her and show her that even though I clearly had suffered some kind of momentary brain damage as I sat there in the truck that I liked her and didn't want our first date to end like this. The only problem was that by the time I stumbled over the hedges I didn't remember being in front of the porch in the daylight and made my way to the door, she'd turned the light out, a clear sign she wasn't holding out hope for me tonight.

But that couldn't be the end of it.

Quickly, I knocked on the metal of the screen door and waited to see the front door open, but as the seconds ticked by and the sound of my heartbeat filled my ears, I knew she wasn't coming back down. She'd given me a chance and I'd ended up being the jackass she always thought I was.

Standing there in the darkness, I wondered if maybe this was who I was with women. No wonder I hadn't remembered my real name and identity yet. Who would want to remember he was an asshole?

No, that couldn't be true. I might not have been that movie star everyone thought I was for about fifteen minutes my third day in Hansonville, but I didn't make people turn to stone with my looks. And even a guy with amnesia could look down his body and see he had some good stuff to offer a woman. Whatever I'd been before I woke up on the side of that road without a clue who I was, I definitely wasn't a loser with women.

In the darkness, I carefully made my way around Clare's house, only tripping over the garden hose once and nearly landing on my face and only slamming my shin into a cinder block one time. Staring up at what I assumed to be her bedroom window, I considered my choices.

I could throw some pebbles up at the glass to get her attention. That could work.

Or I could call up to her. That might work too, but that risked scaring the hell out of her since she'd never heard me yell. Out here in the middle of nowhere, she might think some madman was about to break in.

Neither of those felt right. This needed to be a big move by me but nothing weird that would make her think she needed to pull a gun out and shoot some intruder. As my mind played with the thought that Clare may actually have a gun, I made my decision.

The back porch sat directly beneath her bedroom, so I climbed up on top of its roof and looked up to gauge how I could reach her window. A ledge ran along the second floor of the house, thankfully, so I jumped up to grab it and pulled myself up so I stood directly outside her room. I wiped the sweat from my hairline after my burst of athleticism and took a deep breath.

Lit up by the light on her dresser on the far wall, the room looked like she'd been there but left. Damnit! Did she run down to the front door to answer it? I could have saved myself running through the obstacle course of her yard and climbing up the side of her house if I only waited.

I watched through her window, not missing the fact that when she walked in again, she'd probably freak out when she saw me standing there. I considered moving off to the side, but the last thing I wanted to have to do was knock on her window after she turned off the light.

Christ, none of this was working according to plan! This never happened in any of those fucking Hallmark Channel movies.

Finally, after nearly five minutes, I saw her walk into the room and head toward her dresser. Damn! She planned to turn out the light!

I gently tapped on the glass, hoping not to startle her so she screamed, but she didn't hear me. So I knocked a little harder. Clare looked over toward where I stood, and her eyes grew wide.

"Matt! What are you doing out there?" she yelled as she ran across the room and threw up the window.

"I didn't want to scare you. Honest."

"So you decided to climb up to my bedroom window and knock on it? I think you missed the mark."

"Sorry about that."

Suddenly, my plan to show her how much I liked her seemed ridiculous.

Clare looked out toward where I stood and shook her head. "How did you get up here?"

"I think I might have been a stunt man in my former life, to be honest," I said, forcing a chuckle as I finished speaking.

"Why did you do this?" she asked, finally getting to the heart of the matter.

After I took another deep breath, I smiled and confessed the truth. "I'm sorry I acted like some backwards ass in the truck back there in the driveway. There was nothing wrong. I just didn't want to blow it, but by the time I figured out what to do, you'd jumped out of the truck."

"Blow what?"

I looked through the screen into her blue eyes and hoped she saw my sincerity as I explained myself. "I didn't want to blow my chance with you. I guess that didn't go very well."

She sighed and gave me a sweet smile. "I

thought you decided you didn't like me after our date. I thought you were trying to think of a nice way to tell me you only wanted to be friends."

"No way. I like you, Clare. I more than like you. I don't climb up the side of just anyone's house. I mean, I might, but this is the first time I've done it since I got here to Hansonville."

For a moment, she didn't understand my joke, and then she giggled shyly. "Well, that's good to know."

We stood there looking at one another for a long moment before she said, "I don't usually invite men into my bedroom on the first date, but since you made such an effort, would you like to come in?"

Nodding, I watched as she lifted the screen and stepped back so I could crawl in. This hadn't been a very smooth move, but at least she didn't push me off the ledge.

When I stood up to my full height, I looked around at her room. I wasn't sure what I'd expected, but the pale pink bedspread and picture of her and Emma at the beach in a frame on her nightstand surprised me.

For all her toughness, Clare was a sentimental, feminine woman. I liked that part of her as much as the part I'd seen at the bar tonight.

"I'm impressed that you could climb up to the second floor of my house," she said as she moved to walk around me toward the door.

Catching her by the arm, I gently pulled her to me. "I'd do at least that to show you how much I want to be with you, Clare."

She looked up at me and bit her lower lip. "I want to think you're a good one, Matt. Don't make me regret letting you in."

I knew she meant more than just letting me into her room. She didn't have to worry, though. I wanted to know every incredible part of her, and I had no plans to make her regret a moment of our time together.

CHAPTER ELEVEN

Clare

HE STOOD THERE looking far too sexy for my own good. That's for sure. But how could I not give him a chance after he basically scaled the side of my house to talk to me like some kind of superhero?

For a fleeting moment, I considered being the prim and proper woman most of town would approve of, but as my eyes scanned his body and how good he looked, the thought of not sleeping with him disappeared into thin air. Those stiff townies may let a good thing pass them by, but not me.

"So this is your bedroom?" he said with a chuckle. "Very feminine."

I glanced around the room and shrugged. "I am a female, so that works."

Matt's gaze slowly slid down my body and then back up to my face. With a sly grin, he nodded. "Definitely a female. I like what you sleep in. Not as nice as the dress but even sexier."

Looking down at my blue silk shorts and white T-shirt, I remembered I didn't have a bra on. While the house wasn't chilly by any means since the temperature outside had barely dipped into the seventies and I didn't have air conditioning, my nipples poked through the shirt.

I felt the blush come over my cheeks at the recognition that he likely knew why they were already hard and lifted my head to look at him. "I never thought of this as sexy."

Finally, he stepped toward me and cupped his palms over my shoulders. "Trust me. It's a very sexy look."

With the first touch, it felt like the world stopped turning as I watched him lean down to kiss me. My heart beat rapidly, racing while I waited to feel his lips touch mine. The closer he got, the more I wanted him, and then the moment came and I closed my eyes to revel in our first kiss tonight.

Soft and yielding, it made me feel like I was soaring. I got so lost in how incredible a kisser Matt was that I didn't realize he'd slid his hands under my shirt until his forefinger grazed my nipple.

"Mmmm…." I moaned, eager for this to go to the next level.

"I think it's time we got out of these clothes,"

he whispered before lifting my shirt over my head.

His idea sounded perfect to me, so I reached out and began unbuttoning his pants. Above me, I heard him make a noise and looked up to see a look of surprise on his face.

"I do love a woman who knows what she wants."

As I tugged his zipper down, I smiled. "Good because that's the kind of woman I am. What kind of man are you?"

For a second, he didn't answer, and then he cupped my breasts in his hands and tenderly ran the pads of his thumbs over my excited nipples. "I can't know for sure since that whole amnesia thing, but at this moment, I'm willing to bet some good money that I'm a breast man."

My fingers reached the bottom of his zipper, and behind his underwear I felt the evidence that whatever kind of man he was when it came to women, when it came to men, he was nothing less than blessed.

Gorgeous, well-built, and well-hung? As that thought rushed through my brain, a hint of insecurity rose inside me. No, not that I wasn't pretty enough or any of that. I was twenty-eight years old, so I'd shaken those worries long ago.

My fear grew from a worry that there was no way a man who had all these things going for him could actually be single.

"Earth to Clare? Something wrong?"

Matt's voice ripped me out of my thoughts, and I shook my head. "No. Why?"

As he reached to tug my shorts down my legs, he answered, "Because you seemed to fade out there for a minute. I thought maybe you were having second thoughts."

Not second thoughts but definitely thoughts, to be sure.

I forced myself to smile as genuinely as possible because I didn't want to talk about what I'd just been thinking. Not how I silently had sized up his cock and found it quite impressive, and not how I'd catalogued all his finer attributes women like.

And certainly not that I suspected that even as I planned to sleep with him that he had a girlfriend, fiancé, or wife somewhere in the world I should truly be worried about.

"Nope. No fading I promise."

"Good because I think having the first woman I remember wanting to sleep with suddenly deciding she didn't have any interest could be a mortal blow to my ego."

The way he said that, like he was trying to joke but it didn't quite make it to funny, made me feel rotten. I didn't know if it was my issues or his issues that had gotten into my psyche, but whatever it was, it needed to get the hell out of the way. It wasn't every day a woman had the chance to sleep with a man she liked who had everything going for him Matt did.

I slid my hand inside his pants and palmed his hard cock. "Well, we definitely wouldn't want that to happen. I think being someone's first is special, and although I'm sure I'm not really your first, I'm thinking of myself as that. So crushing your ego doesn't sound very special."

Matt moaned softly and slid my shorts down my legs. "Definitely not special, but I've got a good idea what is."

I stepped out of them, leaving me only in my panties, and turned my attention to his clothes. But before I could help him out of his pants, he took me into his arms and gently guided me down onto the bed.

"You stopped me before I could get you naked," I said with a smile as I looked up at him. God, he was beautiful!

"Don't worry. I'm on top of that," he said and then pushed his pants and underwear down his legs.

As he wriggled his feet out of them, I joked, "I liked you better on top of me, to be honest."

Tossing his pants and then his shirt onto the floor, he turned back to look at me, his eyebrows raised in surprise. "I love that you're the kind of woman who's comfortable making jokes during a time like this. I didn't think you'd be like that."

My gaze travelled down his body, my eyes filling with the view of his muscular chest and washboard abs. We didn't even have a gym in Hansonville. How could he keep himself in such good shape for the past month? Sarah must have had him doing some seriously hard work for his room and board.

Thank you, Sarah. I needed to buy her a coffee the next time I saw her at the Starbucks.

"Like what you see?" he said in a confident tone that made me blush.

"I was just wondering how you stay so buff in a place that has no gym. Do you spend each night doing crunches to get like this?" I asked with a smile as he nudged my legs open wider.

Lowering his head, he nuzzled my neck as his cock pushed against my clit, sending a rush of excitement through me. "I don't do a lot. To be honest, I woke up on the side of Highway 27 like this."

He lifted his head and smiled down at me. "I probably shouldn't say this, but I'm thinking another month in town and I probably won't look like this anymore."

I slid my hands over his powerful back, loving the feel of the corded muscles beneath my touch. Whatever he turned into next month, for now, I planned to enjoy how perfect he was right now.

Dragging my nails across his soft skin, I closed my eyes and moaned as he slid into me, filling me completely and nearly taking my breath away. He remained still for so long that I opened my eyes, and I saw him looking down at me in a way that made me wonder if something was wrong.

"Matt?"

"Yeah."

"Did I do something? You stopped."

"No."

Now I definitely thought something was wrong.

"What's going on?" I asked, afraid all this talk would kill whatever we had going on together.

"I was just looking at you. You're beautiful, Clare."

No man had ever stopped during sex to tell me he thought I was beautiful before. Never. I didn't know what to say in response. Thank you? That didn't seem right.

So I slid my hand around the back of his neck and pulled him down to kiss him long and deep like I'd wanted to since I saw him standing on my porch hours ago looking so gorgeous. His tongue quickly slid over mine, ratcheting up my need for him. I pressed my heels into his lower back and urged him to move once again, and thankfully, he took the hint.

With each thrust of his hips, he touched a

part of me that no man had ever reached. I craved more of him as he fucked me, and soon we fell into a rhythm that felt like heaven. I stopped caring that he didn't know who he was or what his life was away from Hansonville and this room.

Without pausing, he rolled me over so I sat on top of him and smiled up at me. "I thought turnabout would be fair play," he said, punctuating his sentence by lifting his hips so he filled me once again.

"Fair play, huh? Sounds like more work for me," I teased before rolling my hips. "But I'm up for it. Just don't let me see you fold your arms behind your head or things will have to change quickly."

Matt set his hands on my hips and gave them a gentle squeeze. "No resting on the job. Got it. I promise to actively participate."

I rolled my hips once more and leaned down to kiss him. Against his lips, I whispered, "I plan to keep you to that promise."

Sitting back up on him, I moved up and down, undulating so I took all of his cock and then released him and over again as he groaned something about being good as his word. I didn't hear most of it as the sensations of riding him pushed everything but the purest ecstasy out of my consciousness.

There would be time for talking later. Now I

just wanted to enjoy how good he made me feel and do the same for him.

I closed my eyes and let the moment wash over me, and a second later, the feel of his mouth on my breast added another layer of pleasure to what was already incredible sex. I looked down and saw him grin up at me before taking my nipple between his upper and lower teeth.

"Just thought I should join in, and since I've decided I'm definitely a boob man and this was just there waiting for me, how could I not?"

For a few seconds, I watched him toy with me, teasing my tender skin with his lips and teeth, and when it became too much, I stuffed my hand into his hair and tugged his head against me. "Harder. Please," I moaned.

He obliged, and even though I wished it would have taken longer, my orgasm tore through me less than a minute later. Loving how good it felt, I buried my head in the pillow next to his head and bucked my hips over and over as my release rolled over my body.

Matt's hands clamped down on my ass just as I thought it ended and thrust hard into me before coming and setting off a second orgasm for me. Behind my eyelids, it looked like fireworks exploded, bright colors and white flashes of light pulsating as my body rode him through the best release I'd ever experienced.

When we finally stilled, I knew I was in trouble. If he had only been gorgeous, well-built, and hung like a horse but didn't know a damn thing about making love, I would have been safe. Small-town guys routinely didn't know much about sex, other than that they wanted to have it as much as possible. I'd sort of gotten used to mediocre times in bed with boyfriends. Sex wasn't that important, right?

Now that I'd had great sex with Matt, I had to disagree with all those times I'd claimed it didn't matter in a true relationship. Yes, it damn did!

And for that very reason, I knew I'd need to watch my feelings for him didn't get too intense, too quickly. No matter how much I didn't want to focus on the fact that he was a mystery man from somewhere else, that was the truth of who Matt was.

No matter how much I was falling for him.

He gently brushed his fingertips down my spine as he whispered in my ear, "I'm not sure what any other time I've had sex was like, but I damn well hope they were all like that because that felt incredible."

I lifted my head off the pillow and looked down at him. "Always with the amnesia stuff."

Matt flashed me one of his sexy grins. "It's my thing. I can't help it if I think about it a lot."

"Well, it makes me think of things I don't

want to think about," I said more seriously than I wanted to.

Pulling me to him, he pressed a kiss to the top of my head and sighed. "I'm sorry. I promise I won't bring it up again."

I hated hearing the sadness in his voice, so I tilted my head to look up at him. "Then I won't think about it either."

His eyes lit up from his smile at my promise, and he kissed me on the forehead. "I'm going with the motto that sometimes the only thing that matters is the present. I say we both go with that."

As much as that had never been my way of looking at life, I wanted to be that person who thought that way now. He had no past, and I was a woman who didn't want to remember most of hers.

And the future? Neither of us knew what might happen even a day from now, so why not enjoy what we had together at that very moment?

I nodded and rested my head on his chest. I wouldn't let the past ruin things for me this time, and I wouldn't worry about the future.

For the first time in my life, I'd live in the present and let myself enjoy it for what it was. A good time with a gorgeous man who could give me multiple orgasms.

As far as presents went, that was a pretty damn good one.

CHAPTER TWELVE

Clare

WORK THE DAY after felt like my body showed up but my brain got lost in a post-sex haze. Post great sex haze.

I didn't want to admit it, but I felt myself falling way too hard already. Not that I was necessarily regretting sleeping with Matt. As any woman who's had her world rocked will tell you, there's no regretting that.

No way, no how. Even if you want to, memories of how great it felt always made you change your mind.

At noon, Emma called to ask if I wanted to meet for lunch, and it took every ounce of self-control I possessed to not merely blurt out everything swirling around in my brain. It wasn't every day I could honestly report to my best friend that a date hadn't been just good but damn phenomenal.

So at right after twelve, we sat down at one of

the outside tables at Nono's with our slices of pizza and sodas. With the sun shining and not a cloud to mar the perfect blue sky, it seemed like life had finally decided it was my chance to have a shot at the good stuff.

Emma took a bite of her lunch and then a sip of Diet Coke before leveling her gaze on me. I watched her swallow and waited for her to say something, but all she did was stare.

"What? Do I have sauce on my chin? Tell me so everyone walking up and down the street doesn't see I don't know how to manage eating a slice of pizza," I said, feeling defensive suddenly.

"All anyone's going to see looking at you is that you clearly had a good time last night. I thought we were best friends, Clare. You haven't said word one about what happened, but it's written all over your face, so fess up."

I'd seen my friend get sassy with others, especially at her job in the hospital, but she reserved her sassiest outbursts for me, it seemed. Caught off guard, I nearly choked on my soda.

"What do you mean it's written all over my face? What's written on my face?" I asked, sure she heard the guilt in my tone.

Not that I should feel guilty about sleeping with Matt. No, the guilt was that as her best friend since grade school I hadn't told her anything about it yet nearly a day after. We weren't in high school anymore, but best friends shared romance and sex details no matter what age they were.

"That you had a good time. Weren't you listening to a word I said, Clare? Well, other than the written all over your face part."

Emma stopped, and then before I could say a word, her mouth dropped open and she pointed at me. "You slept with him! Now I know why you care what's written all over your face. Oh my God! I thought you guys were just going out to see a bluegrass band."

"How did you know that?" I asked, obviously missing the point of everything else she said just a little too loudly as we sat not ten feet away from a couple having their lunch a few tables away.

"Matt came to me to ask what you like, so I told him penguins, macaroni and cheese, and bluegrass. So he made plans to take you to a bar where you could hear a band play. Now stop beating around the bush and tell me what happened that made a simple first date to a bar turn into sex, and don't leave out any details."

Sheepishly, I took a drink of my soda and cleared my throat. Leaning toward her, I lowered my voice and said, "He climbed up to my bedroom window and when I let him in, I just decided to go for it. Not that he wasn't into it, but for the first time in my life, I did what you always say I should. I went for it."

She clapped her hands together loudly, drawing the attention of the couple nearby, so I quickly slapped her on the wrist. "Stop making so much noise. Someone will hear you."

"Fine, but I'm thrilled that you went for it," she whispered. "Now tell me all the good stuff, or I'm going to start screaming about how you slept with the mystery guy in town."

"You wouldn't!"

"I would and you know it, so spill the beans," she said as she sat back in her chair.

I knew my best friend well enough to know she meant every word, so I swallowed a bite of pizza and told her enough to satisfy her. "He was great, and underneath those T-shirts and jeans he has a banging body. Like I can't imagine he was anything less than some male model before he wound up here in our little corner of the world."

"Good! And I knew he had something fantastic under his clothes, by the way. The guy is the whole package. But what did you mean when you said he climbed up to your room?"

"We got back to the house and things got weird, so I jumped out of the truck and ran into the house. I guess I got a little freaked out. You know me and my insecurities."

Emma rolled her eyes. "Typical Clare."

"I know, but he followed me. When he

knocked on the front door, I didn't get down to answer it quickly enough. So he went around the back of my house and climbed up on top of the porch to get to my window. It was the most romantic thing anyone has ever done, I think."

"He sure does have a touch of the theatrical. No wonder you slept with him," she said with a wicked grin.

"I slept with him because he's gorgeous, Emma. The climbing up to my room thing only helped with that."

"So are you two a thing or what now?" she eagerly asked.

The problem was I didn't know. We'd parted ways this morning when he had to leave to get to work early at the Colonial Inn, but he promised to call. He hadn't, however. I tried not to think that was a bad sign.

"I don't know. Maybe. I just know I wouldn't mind spending more time with him," I said with a smile.

"Well, that's good! I'm just glad you've decided not to pursue your life's goal of being an old maid," she teased.

Rolling my eyes, I tossed a napkin at her. "You know, it's the twenty-first century now. Women can be single. It's not a crime anymore."

She threw the napkin back at me. "Nobody said it was a crime, but you have spent a long time chasing people away. I'm just happy you're giving this guy a chance."

Emma wasn't wrong. I had made a habit of not giving men a chance after Colin. I could argue that I needed the time to forget him, but I didn't bother. I liked Matt enough to let him in a little. Where we'd go from here, I had no idea.

But I liked thinking about it.

I DRIFTED THROUGH the afternoon more lost in daydreams about Matt than focused on work, and by the time I got home, I couldn't help but wonder why he hadn't called me all day. My insecurities had already kicked into high gear, working overtime to make me believe last night had been a one-time thing and he'd moved on, but I didn't want to believe that.

He hadn't called by the time I got ready to make myself dinner, and I found fighting off my anxiety difficult. After taking out the box of stuffing I planned to make with my chicken, I heard a knock on the front door. I hoped it would be Matt, but since we hadn't spoken, I told myself that was just wishful thinking.

And then I opened the door and there he stood in a pair of jeans and a white T-shirt looking like a true sight for sore eyes. Flashing me a sexy smile, he said, "Hey!"

"Hey, what's going on?"

He held up a pan covered with foil and said, "I wanted to surprise you with dinner since I didn't get to treat you last night."

Opening up the screen door, I watched as he walked through. I did love it when people made my life easier, and I didn't want to cook anyway.

Then I got a whiff of what smelled like butter and cheese and asked, "Is that macaroni and cheese?"

He had asked Emma what I liked and she did say she'd told him about my love of that particular dish. Had he brought me that tonight?

Looking back at me as he headed into the kitchen, he smiled. "Yes, it is, in fact. I heard from a little bird it's your favorite."

"Well, I assume that bird is named Emma."

With a chuckle, he nodded. "Yes, I believe that little bird was named Emma."

I followed him into the kitchen where I found him scooping out platefuls for each of us. He looked so at home there that I wondered if he felt as comfortable with me as I did with him.

"I'll have to thank her the next time I see her since I love macaroni and cheese," I said as I grabbed us both silverware and sat down at the table.

He placed the plate in front of me and said, "The lady at the Patriot swears this is the best macaroni and cheese this side of the Mississippi.

While I can't attest to that, I can say it looks like it could be."

I'd always loved the restaurant's recipe for my favorite dish, so I eagerly dug my fork into the food when he sat down. After a few bites, I noticed he hadn't taken any yet.

"Is anything wrong?"

Matt shook his head, but the look on his face told me he was lying. I looked down at his plate and then up at him as he shoveled a forkful of macaroni into his mouth.

"Yum. Really good."

When my plate was almost clear, I smiled at him from across the table and said, "Well, Matt, I think that might be enough for the Best Actor Oscar of the year."

He looked up at me with surprise in his eyes. "Why? What do you mean?"

I knew he struggled to swallow the few bites of macaroni and cheese he tried, and I had to hold myself back from laughing. He was cute. I had to give him that.

"So, I guess you're not a big fan of macaroni and cheese."

"What makes you say that?"

I glanced down at the pile of it left on his plate. "The fact that you ate like a single ounce of it."

"Well, I wasn't really hungry," he claimed,

clearly lying.

"I think it's so cool that you went to all this trouble. It's actually one of my favorite dishes. Not my favorite, but definitely in the top three."

I saw by his expression of disappointment that he realized he'd eaten macaroni and cheese for no reason and regretted it.

"I think there's a little bird I need to have a discussion with."

He lifted his glass and drank nearly all the water in what seemed like on big gulp. "So, what's your favorite dish if it isn't macaroni and cheese?"

I chuckled and answered as I gathered the dishes and set them in the sink. "I'll tell you what. Maybe I'll make it for you another night, assuming we still want to hang out after tonight."

"Why wouldn't we?"

He seemed genuinely confused from what I could read on his face, and I wondered what he was thinking.

I replied frankly and with a shrug, "You never know. We could disagree on something huge, like politics or religion. Maybe that happens and we decide we never want to see one another again. You never know."

Standing from the table, I walked over to the sink and began to wash the dishes. He came up behind me and lightly touched his hands to my hips. "Or we could have mind blowing sex tonight and never want to be apart from one another ever again."

My cheeks heated from what I knew was a deep blush and turned around. Before I could say anything, he kissed me deeply and made my head spin.

Pulling away, I caught my breath and smiled. "You make it hard to say no."

He slid his arms around my waist and stepped toward me so our bodies touched. "Then don't. Let's spend all night doing a repeat of last night."

When he kissed me, any thoughts of saying no faded away, replaced by a sweet ache that settled into me. Only a crazy woman would deny herself another night of great sex with a hot man, and I wasn't that, by any means.

"I like the way you think," I said as I trailed my finger down the front of his shirt.

"Good. So which is it going to be? The kitchen table or on the floor?" He looked down toward our feet and shrugged. "Looks pretty clean."

Since I hadn't mopped my floor in much longer than I wanted to admit, I shook my head. "Definitely not the floor. No way!"

Matt looked over toward the table and smiled. "Then kitchen table it is. Do you care if I do that movie thing they always do and push everything off the top of it?"

I quickly hurried over to grab the ceramic rooster napkin holder that had been my father's and then picked up all the unopened mail I'd left on the far end of the table for the past week. Carrying it all in my arms, I deposited it onto the counter.

"A real spur-of-the-moment kind of girl, huh?" he said behind me.

As much as I wished I could be that person, I wasn't and there was no point in pretending. Turning around to face him, I shook my head. "Something about those scenes in the movies always brought out my OCD side. Better to just clean off the table first."

He pulled me to him and kissed me. With a smile, he said, "That whole spur-of-the-moment thing is overrated anyway."

I didn't want to talk about how I couldn't change being set in my ways, so I slid my hands under his T-shirt, running my palms over his abs and chest. I loved how soft he felt to the touch, especially that thin line of hair that traveled south from his belly button.

Matt made quick work of taking my clothes off, sliding my work polo shirt over my head before focusing on my bra. With a simple click of the center hook, he had it in his hand and tossed it onto the chair nearby.

"Did I happen to tell you I love front-hook

bras?" he asked with a chuckle. "So easy to get off. Now you get those pants and underwear off and I'll take care of my clothes."

"No sexy, slo-mo stripping me and then me stripping you?"

He ripped his shirt off to reveal that beautiful and muscular torso and threw his head back in laughter. "I'm only a fan of the sweeping stuff off the table move. All that slow motion taking off clothes takes too long."

I watched while he stepped out of his pants and realized he didn't have underwear on. "Seems a little overconfident to not wear any underwear today, don't you think?"

Shaking his head, he walked over to me and began nudging my panties down my legs. "I usually go commando. Those underwear I wore last night were only because it was a first date."

Damn. Was there nothing about this man that wasn't pure sex?

As that thought rambled through my brain, Matt lifted me off the floor and positioned me just above his stiff cock. I slid my arms around his neck and clung to him.

"I thought we were doing the whole sex-on-the-kitchen-table thing," I said, confused.

Slowly, he walked us over toward the wall where my cute puppy calendar hung. "Change of plans. As soon as I saw you standing there, I decided to go this route."

The hard wall brushed against my back, and I looked over at this month's calendar dog, a beagle. "Having sex in front of the puppy?"

For a moment, he didn't seem to understand, so I tilted my head to my left toward the picture of the adorable brown and white dog. He turned to look at it and then back at me.

"Too bad, but Snoopy's going to get a show. Maybe he can tell Charlie Brown so he'll have some skills when he finally gets with the little redheaded girl."

I couldn't help but laugh at his humor. God, this man had a way about him that could charm the birds out of the trees.

His mouth covered mine, smothering the words I planned to say to his joking, and he slowly lowered me down so his cock filled me. Our kiss lingered, long and slow, and unlike the first time we had sex, this time wasn't rushed or hurried.

Matt's lips trailed along my jaw to my ear, and he said in a low voice, "You feel like heaven, Clare. I swear to God I could stay like this for the rest of my life and be happy."

Squeezing him to me, I rocked my hips as the same idea filled my mind. I loved how he felt inside me, and if there was a better feeling in life, I hadn't found it.

We moved in tandem, his hips thrusting and my body receiving, back and forth as the two of us slowly inched toward that moment of sweet release. Matt lifted his head and looked into my eyes, and the intensity in them made all those feelings inside me unravel.

I pressed my heels hard into his lower back and sunk my teeth into his shoulder when my release crashed through me. It was pure and real and better than anything I'd ever felt in my life.

Seconds later, Matt came and slouched against me, the two of us sagging against the wall next to the beagle puppy. Nearly breathless, he whispered, "That animal's seen things now. He's a changed dog."

Giggling, I shook my head and smiled. "Poor puppy."

CHAPTER THIRTEEN

Matt

I'D ALREADY BEEN falling pretty hard for Clare, but after sleeping with her twice, any thought of leaving town vanished from my mind. Everything about her drove me wild in the best possible ways. I wanted to feel every part of her over and over again. The desire to spend time with her clouded my mind throughout everything I did in the day. I wanted her underneath me, above me, all of it.

Clare came into my life, and it felt like everything was different because of her. I couldn't imagine not having that sweetness and her unique way of looking at things around me. I didn't want to.

The problem was that I doubted I could stay in Hansonville forever. It had only been six weeks since I arrived there, but in so many ways, it was home. At some point, though, my memory would come back to me. Sometimes I had the sensation of déjà vu when I'd say something or hear a particular song. I had the feeling it was only a matter of time before the past came alive for me again.

Every time that thought popped into my head, I pushed it away. Everything good in my life existed right here in this small town. I had no intentions of giving any of it up any time soon.

I PULLED UP to Clare's house and saw her sitting on the front porch in a pair of white shorts and a black T-shirt. She smiled sweetly as I made my way up the sidewalk, but something in her eyes made me think something was wrong.

Hesitating for a moment, I stopped in front of her on the steps. "Hey, beautiful."

Her smile didn't fade, but as I watched her eyes, I couldn't shake a sense of uneasiness.

"You're kind of dorky, you know that?" she said in a nice enough way.

"Dorky? I don't think so. Aren't dorky guys computer nerds?" I said with a wink.

Clare laughed at my awkward description of just what the hell dorky meant. "That's fair."

Normally when we got together, she couldn't stop talking, but as we stared at each other and I tried to be cool while I leaned against the railing going up the wooden front steps to her house, all I heard were the crickets that seemed to be out early tonight.

Something was definitely wrong.

"So how was work, dear?" I asked, forcing my tone to sound cute.

Clare shrugged. "Same as usual. Mrs. Phillips and her yorkie's sensitive stomach like every Thursday. I think that dog gets more attention to its digestive system than most humans I've met."

Okay. This sounded like the way Clare normally acted. Complaints about yapping dogs and their helicopter owners seemed normal. Maybe I'd misread what I saw in her eyes as I walked up.

"What is it about small dogs?" I asked. "Or maybe it's their overbearing owners?"

"Both. Give me a husky or German shepherd any day," she said with a strange edge to her voice.

"I think I like bigger dogs too. They seem to be lower maintenance," I added, feeling distinctly uncomfortable all of a sudden.

"Do you think you had a dog in your life before you ended up here?" she asked sharply.

Now I knew something was definitely wrong.

"I don't know. Maybe."

Before I could say anything more, Clare stood from her chair and marched past me into the house. I had no idea what she had on her mind, but I intended to find out.

Following her through the front door, I felt

my stomach begin to knot up. I had no true idea what could be wrong, but fighting with Clare made me more unhappy than I'd felt since I arrived in Hansonville. With each step, my insides felt like someone was hollowing them out second by second, and at some point, I'd end up just a shell on the outside with nothing else left.

I found her standing at the sink washing a dish, her back to me like she had nothing more to say. My curiosity overwhelmed my fear, and after a minute of waiting, I spoke first.

"So what's going on?"

Not my coolest way to begin a conversation, but it at least was something.

"Nothing," she said, not bothering to turn around. "Same stuff as usual, I guess."

Every word said less and less. Not good.

Pushing down my unease, I asked, "Is something wrong, Clare? You seem different tonight."

For the longest time, what I said hung in the air like some unwanted gift she'd chosen not to accept. I knew she'd heard me, so why wasn't she answering?

I took a few steps into the kitchen and stopped. Something about the way she stood there with her back to me said she wanted space, as much as it killed me not to wrap my arms around her and give her the kiss I wanted to press onto her earlobe.

"Clare? What's going on? Why aren't you speaking to me?"

She spun around so fast that the water from the dishes she'd been washing flew off her and hit me. Hurt filled her expression, and although I had no idea what was wrong, she clearly had decided to tell me.

I braced for whatever she had to say and hoped I could explain away anything that was bothering her. The problem was Clare wasn't like the rest of the people in town. A nice smile that seemed genuine and some sweet talk worked with them, but she didn't buy that kind of superficiality.

"So you like big dogs, huh? I guess I should have known better to let myself fall for you after we slept together. You know, I accept the fact that we never talked about things, but I don't appreciate being made a fool of, especially by you, Matt."

Her words stung, but even more, they confused the hell out of me. What did liking big dogs over small dogs and everything else she said have to do with us and what we had together? And what did she mean by accusing me of making a fool out of her?

"Uh…well, I do think I like big dogs, but I get the feeling that's not what this is about," I said quietly, taking a single step toward her but stopping when I saw her eyes narrow.

Her wet hands landed on her hips as she shook her head. "Please don't treat me like I'm an idiot. It's insulting."

"Okay. I get that."

It felt like Clare and I were having two different conversations. Neither of them were any good either.

"Kristy Mason came into the vet's today with her Siberian husky. He needed his yearly shots, but all she could talk about was the night she spent at the Colonial Inn this week. We just started sleeping together a little while ago, for God's sake!"

My head spun with every word. We definitely weren't talking about dogs. Who the hell was Kristy, and what did she have to do with Clare and me?

I had the real worry that the second I asked who this Kristy person was that all hell would break loose, but I had no choice. "Clare, I have no idea what you're talking about. Who is Kristy Manson, and why does she matter?"

"Mason!" she yelled, her face quickly turning bright red. "Don't make me explain this, Matt. I already felt like the world's biggest ass when I had to stand there listening to her talk about how much fun she had and how she couldn't wait to get back to the Colonial tomorrow. Seems she's met someone and they're having the time of their lives."

Now it all made sense.

Taking a step toward her, I stopped when she put her hands up in a clear sign that my recognition of what she meant didn't equate her wanting me close to her. "You think I'm the guy she's sleeping with at the inn?"

"Aren't you?" she snapped.

Shaking my head, my mouth dropped open in shock. "Uh, no. I'm not even sure why you'd jump to the conclusion that it's me. Did she say the guy's name is Matt?"

"Of course she didn't. It's a rendezvous. She's not going to be announcing the name of her lover."

The serious way she said lover made me want to chuckle, but I had a feeling if I let even a hint of a laugh slip out she might throw that pot in the dish drainer at me.

"I'm not sleeping with anyone but you, Clare. I've never even met anyone named Kristy in town. Is she new here?" I asked, hoping to defuse the situation before pots and pans began flying through the air.

Anger flashed in her blue eyes. "New here? You're the only new thing in Hansonville, Matt, and you damn well know that. You've been here long enough to know that nobody comes to a small town like this. People only leave."

I held my hands up in surrender in front of me. "Okay, I definitely understand that. But I don't know her, and I swear to God I'm not sleeping with her on the side at the Colonial. I mean, that's where I work. Smart people don't shit where they eat."

Now it looked like flames might shoot out of her eyes at any second. "That's the reason you wouldn't sleep with her? Oh my God! You need to leave right now."

"No! No! All I meant is I wouldn't do that at all. You know I wouldn't do that, Clare. I'm crazy about you. Whoever this Kristy person is sleeping with, it's not me. I swear."

"Her exact words were he's gorgeous with a great body," she said like any of that proved anything.

"Well, I'm flattered that you think I'm the only person in town who could be described that way, but it's not me."

"She said he was a great kisser too, and every time he kissed her, she felt like she was flying."

I took a step toward Clare and gave her a small smile. "Again, flattered, but it's not me. My guess is she's hooking up with some guy from a town nearby who's cheating on his wife. I swear to you that it's not me."

"There's no one else in town who anyone describes as gorgeous with a great body, Matt. Trust me. I've heard those exact words since the day you rolled into Hansonville."

Now she sounded slightly less enraged, which I hoped meant I wouldn't get hit with anything and we might be able to work this out. I stepped forward and reached out for her hand. She didn't pull away when I touched her, so I brought it to my mouth in a kiss.

"I swear it's not me, Clare. I'm flattered everyone seems to think I look good, but I haven't even glanced at a woman since you and I got together. I promise. I wouldn't do that to you. I wouldn't do that to anyone, but I especially wouldn't do it to you."

"Why?"

With one last step, I opened my arms and pulled her into an embrace. She didn't fight against me, and I had a sense when she let out a heavy sigh that she was relieved to be finished with our first fight.

Pressing a kiss to the top of her head, I whispered my answer to her question. "Because I'm crazy about you, Clare. I thought you knew that."

Quietly, she said against my chest, "The way she was talking, I was sure it was you. I felt like someone was yanking the rug out from underneath me, like with every word she was telling me it was you."

I tilted her head back and looked down into her watery blue eyes. "I wouldn't do anything to ruin what we have. I worked too hard to get you to even go out with me to screw it up with this Kristy person. Trust me. You're the only woman I ever think of."

Clare frowned and drew her eyebrows in toward her nose. "You must think I'm such an ass. I was really a bitch back there."

This time, I didn't try to hide my smile. "Just a little jealous, but it looked good on you. Honest."

Shaking her head, she continued to frown. "Jealousy doesn't look good on anyone."

"Well, it gave you a fiery, sexy look I sort of liked. Sort of, except for the fact that I was worried you might throw that pan over there in the dish drainer at me."

She closed her eyes and winced. "You thought I'd throw something at you? That's definitely not sexy."

"Not true. Men love it when women get jealous. It makes us think we're important. It's a huge boost for the ego."

Looking up at me, she rolled her eyes. "I think you're making fun of me, aren't you?"

"Not at all. I like the idea that you would be

unhappy if I went with anyone else. I also like that you wouldn't just tell Emma and think it would blow over. No, in true Clare fashion, you waited for me to come over and patiently led me into your web."

"Now I know you're making fun of me, Matt."

I pulled her to me and kissed her softly on the lips. "Maybe just a little, but I do like that you didn't just let things stew inside you. You thought I'd done something wrong, and you confronted me in your own way. I can respect that. But I swear I would never step out on you, Clare."

She let out another deep sigh and hugged me tightly. "I'm sorry. I guess I just have a bad past when it comes to romance. I shouldn't have jumped all over you, though. That was wrong, so I am sorry."

The memory of what Emma told me about Clare's romantic past ran through my head as we stood there in each other's arms, and I completely understood why she could be so distrusting of me. We hadn't been together for long, and I could only imagine how bad it must have felt like to have to stand there while some woman described sleeping with someone she thought was devoted to her.

"You don't have to be sorry for anything," I said softly against the top of her head. "I'm flattered that when you hear of a gorgeous man that you think of me first."

She looked up at me and smiled for the first time since we walked into the house. "I think you're starting to get a big head about that. Must be nice to be the best looking guy in town."

"You do know it's not hard in this town. Every other guy is either nearly a senior citizen or a teenage boy. But you know what? I think if I heard anyone describing a beautiful brunette with gorgeous blue eyes, I'd think they must be talking about you, so it's sort of the same."

For a moment, she didn't say anything, but then she just rolled her eyes. "I think you're one hell of a sweet talker, Matt."

"Maybe, but I'm your sweet talker."

And no matter what else I said or how much truth anything I said contained, that was the truest thing I'd ever said to her. I was hers.

And what made me the happiest guy in Hansonville was that Clare was mine.

CHAPTER FOURTEEN

Clare

THE MONTH THAT followed my jealous outburst was one of the happiest I'd ever had in my whole life. Spending time with Matt made me feel like I bloomed into the person I'd always believed I could be. I laughed more, hugged more, felt more than I ever had.

Had I allowed myself to feel the way I had when the last handsome man who came to town swept me off my feet? No. I could never allow myself to get hurt like that again. I couldn't open myself up to a world of pain like that.

At least I tried not to.

Matt made that difficult, though. Overnight, it seemed, he became the most important part of my life. Most days, I would get out of work around five thirty, and by the time I got home fifteen minutes later, Matt would be waiting on the front porch with that sexy smile for me.

Sometimes we'd make dinner, while others

days we'd practically run upstairs to jump into bed, stripping all the way up to my room. Then other times we would walk around the yard and talk and he'd listen to me go on and on about my day and the crazy dog and cat parents who came into the vet's office. He had his own stories about the people he met working at the Colonial Inn, like the man who checked in and asked to have all the pictures removed from the walls of his room one day because he claimed the people in them were trying to talk to him.

He found things like that charming. To me, it just screamed of the bizarre. But that wasn't the main issue I had with the people I'd lived around all my life. Their relentless need to be in everyone's business never suited me. The less I knew about people the better. I hated walking into places like the Patriot and hearing unending gossip about whatever young girl got pregnant or whatever old man had gotten in trouble at work. It felt intrusive hearing about things like that, and yet they insisted on prattling on like little hens.

"Have you ever considered moving? There's a great big world out there. You might like going to a new place," Matt offered one evening as we were eating the honey mustard chicken and green beans we'd made for dinner.

I thought about his suggestion and shrugged. "This is my home. All of my memories are here.

They aren't all good, but they're mine."

The truth was that I had never fully considered moving away. Not really. I went to college locally, about thirty minutes away, and had only taken enough classes to come back and work as a vet tech. I liked my job, and I liked my house. And Emma lived in Hansonville. Before that it had been my father. My leaving him behind and running off to the big city would have crushed him. He would have supported me. I never doubted that for a second, but how could I leave a man so broken alone with nothing but his misery?

So I stayed, and it had never been a decision I'd regretted. If I was supposed to leave Hansonville, the circumstances would present themselves. At least that's what I always told myself.

"Well, take it from someone who knows, sometimes making new memories can be a really great adventure."

I chuckled, but a part of me felt sad for Matt. He had found a new life, but he still didn't even know his real name. Every so often, he seemed to have a glimmer of a memory, but then it would fade as quickly as it came. It never got him down, even if it bothered me because I couldn't deny I wanted to know who he really was.

But then when we lay together in each other's

arms, I knew I already did.

One night we sat on the couch in my living room watching an episode of some show Emma had convinced me was a must watch when he'd kissed me lightly on the neck and whispered, "I love you."

I froze for a moment, my body tensing up and a chill inching its way down my spine. I wasn't scared because Matt had just told me he loved me. I was scared because of just how easily my reply formed in my head.

"I love you too."

And then neither of us said anything for a few minutes. Of course, my brain took that as an invitation to conjure up a thousand ideas about what could be wrong about saying those three words.

Turning to look at Matt, I asked, "Do you think things are moving too fast? I'm worried we'll get burnt out on one another if we keep this up. And is it too soon for, you know, what we said?" The words spilled out of my mouth all at once and I knew I sounded idiotic, but I needed to know.

"I think things are happening at exactly the right pace for us, Clare," Matt said with such sweetness in his voice. "We aren't on anyone else's schedule but our own. Besides, who says people need to know one another for a lifetime before they know how they feel about each other? If we know now, that just gives us more time to enjoy it."

I couldn't help wanting to believe his idea about not being on anyone's schedule for love but ours. Leaning my head on his shoulder, I slid my fingers through his.

"No schedule. I like that."

Closing my eyes, I let go of all those questions and worries. We had the rest of our lives and nothing to do but enjoy each other.

MATT MOVED AGAINST me, and I woke up to see him getting dressed to leave. "Going somewhere?"

He smiled down at me as he slipped his shoes on. "I've got to be up early to help Joe at the inn. I guess someone is getting married there tomorrow, and they need everyone to handle it. I can't stay here with you, or I won't get any sleep."

"A wedding? Anyone local?"

I hadn't heard anything about one, and normally if someone local was getting married, it would've been the talk of the town.

Matt shook his head. "No, not from what I heard. Sarah was complaining that our town isn't just some wedding album backdrop, but Joe reminded her how much they paid and she seemed to be okay with it."

I had to chuckle at how Sarah always gave in

to the bottom line. "My father loved how business savvy Sarah always was. She was kind too, though. When my mother left, I guess Joe and Sarah brought him food. They're good people. I'm not surprised they took you in."

"I'm everyone's favorite stray, I guess," Matt said with a sigh. "But you're right. They're good people."

"Well, have fun tomorrow. I've got some errands to run and I'm having lunch with Emma."

We hadn't been able to meet up for lunch much for weeks since we'd both been busy. I missed my best friend. I had loads to catch up with her about too.

"Tell her I say hello. I'll see you for dinner tomorrow?"

"Don't we do that every night?" I asked as I stood up from the couch.

He pulled me into his arms and kissed me. "Yes, but I like to keep you on your toes, so I keep asking."

I loved that he still asked.

✧   ✧   ✧

SATURDAYS WERE A day off, so I had to head to the grocery store and post office, but a lunch date with my best friend was long overdue and at twelve sharp I walked into the Patriot to meet Emma.

When we'd talked earlier that morning, she'd sounded decidedly chipper, and I realized immediately when I walked up to the table that she'd been holding out on me.

"Oh my God, Emma!" I said as I sat down across from her and checked out her new look so different from usual. "How much did you get cut off?"

She tugged on the ends of her hair that hit just at her shoulders. "I think the stylist said about eight inches. What do you think?"

Her long hair she'd worn for over a decade was gone, switched out for a no-nonsense bob. It completely suited her.

"Emma, you look amazing! What made you decide to do it?"

"Well, this morning I was trying to brush my hair and it was so tangled because I didn't condition it yesterday like I should have. So it was taking me forever and my arm was getting tired and that was it. When I finally got the brush through it, I marched down to the salon and told her to cut it all off. She talked me out of getting it cut short, but now it won't be a problem brushing it. No one likes finding their nurse's hair on the charts or in their bed anyway. Do you really like it?"

"Honestly? I love it. It frames your face perfectly!"

It did too.

"How does it feel? Do you feel lighter?"

"So much lighter. It's like I lost five pounds off my head. I don't miss it, though. Maybe I will on days when I want a ponytail, but it's just hair. It'll grow back if I want it to."

"Exactly, but I think you should keep it this way. It's a great new look."

Emma beamed a smile at my compliment as she tugged on her hair again. "I'm going to. So enough about me? What's new with you and Mr. Dreamboat? I feel like I've hardly seen you lately. When was the last time we did lunch, like three weeks ago? You better not let this guy steal you from me," she teased.

"Not much is new. In his defense, I've been crazy busy at work. The other girl, Alison, had her baby and she decided during her maternity leave that she wasn't coming back. They're trying out this whole new schedule that means I have to work more hours. If it works, I get a salary bump, though."

"Has it been hard getting used to?"

"Yes and no. It's a lot at once, but it does have me there from about nine to six most days and I'm taking lunch at my desk. It'll even out once I'm used to it, but for a couple months it'll be hectic."

We stopped talking to give our waitress our drink orders. When she walked away, Emma said, "You've got this. Is there any way I can help?"

"Not really, unless you want to bring me lunch some days. Living off sandwiches is getting boring."

She laughed and nodded, "Totally! You've been doing that for me for the longest time. Time to switch it up. I get lunch, see my best friend, and get away from the hospital. Done deal."

My best friend studied my face for a long moment. "So enough deflecting. Tell me about lover boy."

I blushed at her mention of Matt and took a sip of my drink. "He's good. You know how it is."

My vague answer did nothing to ease her curiosity. "I do know how it is, but I'm wondering why you aren't giving me the details."

I shrugged and smiled. "I'm not sure what you want to hear."

Emma threw her head back and laughed. "Oh man, you're in love with him, aren't you?"

I bit my lower lip and hedged before nodding slightly. Emma didn't react in quite the same reserved way as I had.

She clapped her hands and giggled before saying far too loudly, "Matt and Clare sitting in a tree. K-I-S-S-I-N-G!"

"Oh Emma, hush," I said as my cheeks heated up from embarrassment. "It's not that big a deal."

"Not that big a deal? Clare, you haven't felt like this for anyone since…"

Her sentence trailed off, but I knew where she'd been going and finished her sentence for her.

"Since Colin. I know. And that's why I'm not trying to rush into anything or get my hopes up."

I didn't want to think about how things had gone in the past. Emma knew not to bring him up, but I was adult enough not to break down over it after six years. Still, the memory was ever present and sharp, like a thorn in my side.

"Clare, are you happy?"

"Honestly? Yes, I really am. He makes me feel amazing and I'm not just talking about in bed. I'm just scared that…"

Emma waved her hand. "Stop that! Stop being scared! You've been petrified for six years, Clare. Let yourself be happy."

"I know. We actually told each other we loved each other last night, and it didn't take even ten minutes before I was worried we were going too fast."

"What did he say about that?"

"That we weren't going too fast. That we were going at just the right speed. But you know how I am. I wish I was more like Matt and you. Both of you guys are so fearless when it comes to stuff like this."

She shook her head and smiled. "I bet he's not fearless, and I'm definitely not. We just look at things differently."

"Do you think you would be that way if you had a Colin in your past?" I asked, hoping I wasn't some kind of pathetic thing that would forever be haunted by that romance that had gone so wrong.

"Probably not. I don't think you should feel that way either, though. Not anymore. You and Matt have been spending time together all summer, and it's obvious you're happy. Let yourself enjoy that for once."

Since I'd never held back the truth from Emma, I leaned toward her and quietly spoke the words that never truly left my mind. "But what about when he gets his memory back?"

She took a deep breath in and sighed. "I know. I've thought of that more than once, but you know what? Not a single person has even tried to find him this whole time. I don't think there's anything you have to worry about. Maybe he's just the man he seems to be."

On my way home, I thought about what she said and knew she was right. Sometimes all it took was hanging out with Emma to help my perspective. She had a way of understanding things about relationships. Maybe it came from being a nurse, or maybe she just had a sense of what was real.

I poured myself some iced tea and sat down on the porch in the afternoon sun to relax. Closing my eyes, I let all my worries go.

A soft touch on my skin roused me, and I woke to Matt kissing me gently on the forehead. "Hey, pretty lady. Don't you know it's not safe to fall asleep out here?"

Wiping the sleep from my face, I smiled up at him. "This is Hansonville. I could fall asleep in the middle of the road and still be safe. People would just drive around me."

"Want to stay in for dinner, or do you feel like traveling tonight?"

"Let's stay in. I can make something with the chicken I bought today."

Matt extended his hand and pulled me up from my seat. "How about I cook for you tonight? Just give me the recipe and I'm on it."

"Sounds good," I said, and we walked inside together. It felt natural, being there in my home and making dinner with him.

As he got all the ingredients together to make honey garlic chicken, I watched in awe that I had such an incredible person in my life. Emma was right. I needed to let myself be happy.

Flashing me a smile, he stirred the fragrant

honey garlic sauce at the stove and said, "I really do love you, Clare. Just in case you forgot."

"I love you too. And I didn't forget."

I never wanted to forget exactly how wonderful sitting there in my kitchen with Matt felt. For the first time in six years, I could honestly say I believed I could be happy with someone again.

CHAPTER FIFTEEN

Matt

EVERY DAY FELT better than the one before it. Clare and I were in love, and we were building something bigger than us together. I woke up to her beautiful face most days and made love to the woman I adored. I'd even started to move some of my things out to her house.

Life was good.

Then, one night in August, reality called. Literally.

As I headed toward the stairs to walk up to my room at the Colonial Inn, my arms full with a basket of my clean clothes straight from the laundromat, I saw the front desk clerk Misty wave toward me.

"Matt, someone called earlier for you and left her name and number and asked that you call her back as soon as possible."

She handed me the folded-up piece of hotel stationary that had the caller's note on it. I thanked her before rounding the corner and heading back to my room where I could use the phone there. No one knew my room number, so it was no surprise that they'd left the message with the front desk, but who had called?

Maybe John's wife had invited me to dinner? She had said she wanted to, but that was a few months ago. But I just saw her yesterday and she didn't say a word about any invitation.

My hand shook as I sat down on the bed and opened the note, trying to ignore what my gut was telling me. Not more than a few words in and my heart sank into my stomach.

How the fuck had Sierra found me?

I picked up the hotel phone on my nightstand and dialed her number as my chest began to ache. It barely rang once before I heard, "Hey, about time you got back to me. We've got a situation."

Sierra's sharp voice pierced the final remnants of happiness inside me, and I sighed. "How did you find me?"

"How do you think I found you?" she asked like my question didn't require an answer.

I guessed it didn't. This wasn't the first time she'd had to find me in some far flung place in the world. Sierra did her job well. That's why I paid her so fucking much. It's just that this time, I wished she wasn't so efficient.

"What's the situation?"

I didn't want to talk to her. I didn't want everything to be over. I knew the moment I saw her number on the paper that everything I'd built up over the last few months had already begun to crumble.

But I didn't want to let it go. Not yet. I wanted just a little longer. Another kiss. Another night making love to Clare. It couldn't be over. Not yet.

I knew the truth, though. If Sierra was calling, my time was up. She'd found me, and now I'd have to leave Hansonville and the woman I loved.

"You're not going to like it. The stand-in guy got into some trouble here in LA. Your little secret is going to be big news on every major news station tomorrow morning. I get that you needed to escape, but the jig is up. I need you on the next flight out of that Podunk town and back here in LA."

Cringing at that word—Podunk—I hated how she referred to Hansonville. I hated her and this news and her for being the one to give it to me. I hated everything about the situation I had just been thrust into.

"Wait, what do you mean the stand-in got into trouble?" I asked, hoping to grab just a few more days to make things right.

All the information she was throwing at me was so sudden, but I needed answers. Sierra, however, refused to give them, and shot back, "Listen to me. I've got a fixer handling everything. It's all going to be fine, but only if you're front and center here tomorrow. Do you understand?"

She never used that tone with me unless things were really bad.

"Sierra, just call it off. Call it all off."

I didn't want to pretend anymore. I could fix things myself and make a new life in Hansonville with Clare.

"What do you mean?" she asked in astonishment, as if not returning to LA sounded like lunacy.

Of course, it would to her. She hated small towns. I'd done a few shoots in small towns back when I was doing television, and she'd always refused to come see me, even when she needed to. If she wasn't in a big city, she turned into a panicked mess. In that chaos, she found some sort of peace, something I never understood.

"You heard me. Call the whole thing off. I don't want to come back this time. I've found something here. Something good. I'm staying here. I'm not going back to that old life."

Sierra sighed, and I imagined her doing that thing where she rubbed her temples as she tried to work through her irritation with me. She'd said a million times that I was her most pain in the ass client. Funny how the scads of money I made seemed to make up for that.

Finally, she said, "Honey, this something good that you found? Is she going to be okay with the lies?"

I didn't want to answer that. I didn't want to face that reality yet. I couldn't. Everything was unraveling so quickly and I felt like I was gasping for air as it was. Facing that was not an option at the moment.

Even if I knew the answer. No, Clare wouldn't be okay with the lies.

Sierra continued, "What happened to you? You dropped off the radar like I had a feeling you planned to, but how did you end up in that small town in Pennsylvania two weeks later?"

"I hitchhiked across the country, and things were going fine until two guys picked me up and mugged me."

"You're lucky they didn't go to the tabloids that day," she said with more than a hint of disappointment, like she wished they had.

A chuckle escaped from my throat. "I don't think they knew who the hell I was. They just wanted money. That's what I get for getting into a van with them."

"So they dumped you off in the middle of nowhere and you just decided to make a life there?"

"Not exactly. They knocked me out and left

me on the side of the road. When I woke up, I had no idea who I was."

Sierra laughed into the phone. "So that call from that doctor that day was for real? I thought you were acting, but you really had amnesia? I just figured you needed some time away, so I played my part and acted like Marco Randolph was in the south of France. I had no idea you were holed up in some rinky dink hospital not knowing who you really were."

"It's not that bad here. Stop acting like it's some hole in the wall place where only people with one or two teeth hang out."

"So this something good you say you found. How long have you been lying to her?"

Christ, I hated hearing her say it like that. I never meant to lie. I didn't know who the hell I was, so maybe I shouldn't have started anything with Clare, but it didn't begin as a lie.

Even if it did morph into one.

From the moment my memory began to slowly come back to me, I wished that I really could forget my life and just settle down in Hansonville. For far too long, I'd been a man walking around pretending to have amnesia wishing he could truly have amnesia.

How quintessentially Hollywood.

"So you lied to this woman the whole time? Do you think she's going to be okay with that?"

"It wasn't the whole time," I mumbled as I closed my eyes and leaned back onto the bed.

"No answer to that?" Sierra continued. "Well, let me explain something to you about women. Unless she's some unicorn kind of person that I doubt exists, she's going to be pissed. She thinks she fell for some guy who has no memory of his old life, when in truth, she fell for a guy who lied to her for months."

I quickly corrected her. "It wasn't months. Just weeks."

"Oh, okay. As if that makes a difference. I know women, Marco. Trust me. She's not going to be okay with this. It doesn't matter how sexy you are or how sweet you are. You lied to her. For weeks. That's all she'll see."

My head began to throb from a headache. Was Sierra right? I'd convinced myself that everything would just work out. It always had. Why wouldn't it now? For the first time in my life, I'd found real love. It had to work out.

"I just wanted a break from the crazy LA scene. Why the hell is that so wrong?"

"Nobody said that was wrong, honey. But you lied to her. You can dress this up any way you want. You lied. Trust me. Women hate that."

"I didn't want to ruin everything once I remembered who I was. To be honest, I never intended to fall in love. That just sort of happened."

Sierra sighed, but this time it sounded less like one of exasperation and more like one of pity. "You can tell her all of that and she's still only going to hear that you lied, Marco. I wish I was wrong. Maybe I am. Maybe this will turn out okay. I hope it does."

Jesus. How was I supposed to look the woman I loved in the eye, a woman who'd been hurt by lies before, and tell her I wasn't the man I pretended to be for the past few weeks? I loved her. Couldn't that be enough?

I didn't want to listen to my manager anymore. Sierra may have been right, but it all sounded a little too preachy for my taste. She had a habit of doing that. But I didn't want to keep hearing about what a liar I was.

In a tone terse enough to let Sierra know the time for her opinion on the matter was over, I said, "Sierra, say nothing until I contact you again. Do your job and keep the press at bay. Understand?"

I was intentionally sharp with her and she knew damn well that meant I'd reached a place where I couldn't be argued with. Sierra had always been tough on me, and I liked that. But she knew where the boundaries were.

Her answer was curt, the way I liked her. "Yes, Marco."

She hung up, and I stared up at the cracked ceiling paint with the phone still pressed to my ear, left in the oppressive silence of my room. A room that had been given to me free of cost by two people who believed I needed help. Who had trouble keeping their inn afloat while my bank account overflowed.

Punching the pillow next to me, I threw the phone receiver toward the nightstand. Everything was unraveling and I knew I needed to get ahead of it in the only way I had available.

I had to tell Clare before she found out some other way.

I grabbed my keys and ran down the stairs, nearly running into Sarah on the way. With a gentle waggle of her eyebrows, she said, "Oh, off to see that lovely lady of yours?"

But today, instead of feeling thankful for her kind and motherly nature, I just felt the guilt of lying to her and her husband and probably costing them money. They had been good to me, and I felt that pressure of the truth hanging over me now.

I nodded quickly in her direction and ran out of the inn before anyone else could stop me. Better not to see another Hansonville resident and have to lie to them again.

Out on the street, I stared at the truck I was about to drive out to Clare's. The one given to me for free by another kind person in a town I had lied to. I shook my head to push that thought away and got into the truck. I couldn't stand around feeling bad about what I'd done right now. I needed to get to Clare before anyone else did. Thanks to the internet and everyone having information instantly on their phones, nothing stayed hidden long. My secrets were about to unravel in front of a whole town, and Clare would be hit with the brunt of what I'd done.

I had to make sure I got to her before that happened.

As I pressed my foot to the gas pedal and sped down Main Street, I wondered if maybe Sierra was wrong. Maybe Clare would understand what happened and forgive me. I sighed as I hoped against hope for that and ran my hand through my hair as the light at the corner of Main and Chambers turned red.

Goddamned stop lights! Hansonville had a total of three of them, and I'd probably hit every damn one of them today. I just wanted to get to Clare's quickly before she heard this from anyone else, but I also wanted to be suspended in a moment in time where we were fine and none of the truth had to come out. If she could just see past the fib that I told, she'd be able to see that this wasn't a terrible thing.

I was famous and wealthy. I could give her

any kind of life she could dream of. She was never a fan of Hansonville that much anyway, so why wouldn't she want to run off to California with me?

The light turned green, and I jumped on the gas again, ready to run through the next two lights if they turned red. I tore up the street and turned onto Highway 27, the trees flying past me in a blur as I sped toward her house.

Time wasn't on my side. If Sierra was giving me a heads up, I didn't have much time. She was one of the best managers around, but not even a miracle worker like Sierra could keep me safe and insulated forever.

I pulled up to Clare's and skidded to a stop in her driveway. For a minute, I stared at the front porch remembering how many times she and I sat together watching the fireflies. It had been a perfect summer. She'd been perfect.

Now reality threatened to rip it all away from me.

I couldn't let that happen. No. This had to work out.

Horrible scenarios of Clare knowing that I lied and kicking me out of her life forever filled my head. She'd be done with the liar who made her believe love could be real again only to have it taken away from her even worse than before.

That couldn't be the end of us. I wouldn't let

it be. Then again, maybe Sierra was wrong. She didn't know Clare. She only knew LA people. Clare wasn't superficial or vapid. Maybe she'd be understanding. That lying about knowing who I really was didn't mean I loved her any less.

She walked in front of the living room window and I watched her hurry toward the kitchen, probably to stop lunch from burning on the stove. Always so sweet, she probably planned on surprising me with a grilled cheese sandwich in that cute way she had about her.

I wanted that life, and she was the woman I wanted to spend that life with. I had no doubts about it. But that could only happen if she understood I never meant to lie to her.

She'd never fit in with the rest of Hansonville. She knew it, I knew it, and everyone in that town knew it. I could be her escape. All it would take would be her deciding to be understanding and forgiving.

Taking a deep breath, I crossed my fingers and stepped out of the truck. The walk to her front door felt like it had grown to the size of two football fields since I was there yesterday. The oak trees in her front yard seemed to ache and moan as if they knew my misdeeds.

Shooting them a look, I grimaced. I never meant to hurt anyone. I planned to fix everything anyway.

She just had to listen to me. All she had to do was hear me out and she'd understand and everything would be okay. That's what I told myself as I dragged my body up the stairs to knock on her door.

I stood there in the hot summer heat feeling the opposite of what I felt when I knocked on that door so many times. She'd told me over and over that I didn't have to knock, but I did every time, and each time I eagerly waited to see her beautiful face when she opened the inside door.

Now, as much as I wanted to see Clare, I dreaded what expression she'd wear when she saw me.

I raised my hand like life had suddenly turned into a slow motion scene and knocked my knuckles off the metal part of the screen door. A few seconds later she opened the door and smiled at me, happy and hopeful, the way she always did.

"You know, I keep telling you this, but you don't have to knock. Come in!"

Stepping into her house, I felt like my legs had suddenly become encased in concrete. Heavy and slow, they seemed to drag as I followed her into the living room while she talked about what she was making for lunch and some infomercial salesman tried to sell copper pots and pans on the TV.

"Emma told me about this chicken and

broccoli recipe she saw in one of those magazines at the hospital, so I thought I'd try that today. It's a lot for lunch, but we can save some for dinner, if we want. I can't believe I've never seen it since I thought I'd read every one of those ancient magazines cover to cover by now."

When she turned around to look at me as we walked into the kitchen, all I wanted to do was take her in my arms and somehow find a way for the two of us to run away to a place where there was no Marco Randolph, no lies, and no chance that this might be the last time I ever got to be near Clare.

CHAPTER SIXTEEN

Clare

"JUST GIVE ME a minute and lunch will be ready. Grab the iced tea, okay?" I said as I turned off the front burner and gave our meal one last stir.

I scooped up a serving of the chicken and broccoli onto each plate, along with a side of white rice. Turning around, I saw Matt sitting at the table staring at me. He hadn't gotten the iced tea out and looked almost lost.

"Hey, what's wrong? Didn't you hear me say to grab us something to drink?"

He shook his head and gave me a tepid smile before quickly jumping up to head to the refrigerator. "Sorry. I'll get it now."

"Something happen at work? You look like you've seen a ghost," I said as I set our plates down and took my seat across from him.

"No. Nothing happened."

I didn't know what was wrong with him, but

he wasn't acting like himself today. Normally, he and I talked a lot when we sat down to eat together, laughing at something he saw in town or joking around about something I wanted to do with the house that inevitably would mushroom into a huge project.

But today he seemed sullen and distracted.

"Oh, okay. Well, dig in and let me know what you think. Emma raved about it, but then again, I've heard her go wild over tacos from the Patriot and those are definitely not anything to write home about."

I was practically starving, so it wasn't until a couple minutes later that I noticed Matt hadn't touched his food. In fact, by the way he sat biting his fingernails, I wondered if he didn't even like the smell of the food.

It did have a heavy garlic smell to it, even though I only put in one clove. Maybe he didn't like garlicky food on a hot day?

All of this ran through my mind, making my stomach knot up so I couldn't eat another bite until we got whatever it was straightened out. Pushing my plate away, I wiped my mouth and sighed.

"Okay, let's have it. Something's wrong, so let's just talk about it."

Matt's expression morphed into one full of pain. "Nothing's wrong."

"Well, tell your face because it hasn't gotten the memo," I said with a smile, hoping to lighten the mood a little.

My attempt at humor didn't work.

He looked tense, like he had to struggle to keep every muscle in his body still. I'd never seen him in such a state before. Was he angry?

Then out of the blue, his expression softened. "I love you."

"I love you too. Is there something wrong with your food?"

"No. It's great. I just, I really love you, Clare. You know, that right?"

I frowned as I nodded and repeated, "I love you too. What's going on? I can tell something is wrong and don't just say that you love me. I know you do. Just tell me what's wrong."

He said nothing, but the stress practically radiated off him. What could be the problem?

Then it suddenly hit me. "Does this have something to do with your memory? Are things from your life coming back to you?"

My biggest fear felt like it had finally come to be. He finally remembered who he was and didn't know how to tell me our time was over. I saw him slowly nod, and my heart sank into my stomach.

Oh, God.

The fact that he wouldn't say something and answer me felt like torture. "So, you're remembering life before your accident."

Still no answer. I stood up, my legs shaking with each step I took toward him. Leaning down, I kissed him and said the words that scared me to death. "Okay, so how bad is it?"

A million thoughts ran through my head. Was he married? Engaged? Did he have a family and some office job with a desk where he wore a tie? I could handle a lot of things, the office job and tie included, but if there was something, or someone, in his life waiting for him to return, then we would never be able to continue being together. I couldn't volunteer to ruin someone's life like that.

He gazed up at me, and I remembered that night we had our first date how I thought I could drown in those deep brown eyes of his. He said nothing but bit his lip before looking down at the table.

Okay. Stay calm, Clare.

Whatever he remembered, it was bad for us. If his memories were only about what he liked to do on weekends or that he enjoyed beer a whole lot more than he knew in the past few months, he'd tell me.

I began to ask again if it was bad when I heard someone on the TV mention something that caught my attention. "Breaking news out of Hollywood tonight. A man who everyone thought was Marco Randolph was arrested this evening for soliciting sex in Hollywood. Bad boy Marco starting to sound more like his friend, Ollie, it seems! But here's the twist! Turns out Marco Randolph has been hiding out in our very state! That's right, blockbuster actor Marco Randolph has been hiding out in a little town called Hansonville here in Pennsylvania since June!"

The news anchor went on to say something about my small town, but I couldn't hear anything else. I'd heard the first half and that was enough. I recognized the name Marco Randolph. That's who they thought Matt was that day in the hospital. Emma had said that name over and over in a half hours' time, and there he was sitting in front of me.

I stood up straight and ran into the living room just in time to see the proof for myself. "Here we have a side by side comparison of a picture a local man took recently of the man in Hansonville next to the real Marco Randolph. As you can tell, it's him."

Through teary eyes, I stared at the picture of Matt standing next to his truck in front of the inn. The picture next to it showed him at some party dressed in a designer suit that looked like it cost thousands of dollars, but there was no escaping the truth.

Matt was Marco Randolph.

I stumbled back and fell onto the couch. Matt

walked into the living room a moment later, and I saw the guilt written all over his face.

How long had he known?

"You're Marco Randolph," I said quietly as I inspected his face. "When did you remember who you really are?"

I'd looked at his face so many times before through eyes full of love, and yet now it seemed strange and foreign to me. The jawline covered in stubble I'd touched with my fingertips and my lips so many times. The beautiful mouth that had kissed me and smiled at me all summer. The warm brown eyes I got lost in whenever he looked at me.

Now it felt like a stranger stood in front of me.

A look of shame settled into his features before he looked down at the floor. "It's true. I'm him."

"How long have you known?" I asked as every last ounce of moisture in my mouth felt like it turned to dust.

He looked up at me again, his eyes now pleading. "I can explain. I know how bad this looks, but if you just give me the chance to explain I promise it all makes sense in the end."

I shook my head, a thousand memories we shared over the last two months rattling around my brain. "Why won't you tell me how long you've known? Did you know the whole time?"

"No!" he said as he shook his head. "Not the whole time. I swear."

"Then how long?"

I didn't know what length of time had to do with any of this. That he knew at all any time since he and I began dating meant he'd been lying to me at some point about the most important part of him.

Sheepishly, he avoided my stare and mumbled, "A couple weeks. It just came to me one day, and I knew who I was."

"Why didn't you tell me? Why did you spend weeks lying to me?" I asked, wishing so much that none of this bothered me.

"Clare, listen, it wasn't like that. I just wanted some time away from my life, and when it came back to me who I was, I remembered it was all too much. Too many parties. Too many relationships. Too many nights I wanted to forget. I knew I loved you, so I wanted to stay here and be that guy with the great life with you."

I thought when Colin left that I knew what deception felt like, but it turned out the world had just given me a taste before the full course a few years later. How could I have let myself fall for another handsome man who came to town?

No. I shook my head. This wasn't my fault. I wasn't the wrong one here.

Matt. No, Marco, rushed over to kneel in front of me and reached out to take my hand, his fingers gently brushing the top before I jerked it away furiously.

"Clare, I swear I never meant to lie. I didn't know who I was when they found me out on Highway 27. Then everyone in town turned out to be so nice that when I remembered the truth I didn't want to leave Hansonville. None of that was a lie."

"Just everything between you and me for the past few weeks, I guess," I snapped, interrupting his explanation.

He clutched my hand and kissed it. "No! I swear that's not true. I fell in love with you, and then when I remembered who I was, I didn't want to ruin things between us. LA has a way of doing that to a person, and I didn't want to lose you. So I stayed here because I didn't want us to end."

"You lied to me, Matt." As soon as that name left my mouth, I shook my head at how wrong it sounded now. "I don't even know your real name."

"What does it matter? I've known for weeks who I was and that didn't change the fact that every time you called me Matt it was who I was."

I opened my mouth and then closed it, unsure what to say to that twisted logic. A name meant everything. It was who you were in the purest sense.

"Why can't you see what you've done? It was all a lie," I said and hung my head, too sad to keep saying the same thing.

But he moved so I had to see his face looking up at me, unable to escape the pain in his dark eyes. "It wasn't all a lie. Only the last few weeks I knew, but I wasn't really lying. I never lied when I said I loved you. I never lied when you asked me what I wanted to eat or if I liked what you were wearing. Why does it matter so much that I have a different name? Matt, Marco. It doesn't matter."

"You made me believe you were someone you weren't. You let everyone think they were helping some poor soul who had no idea who he was. You lied to good people. I'm not just talking about me. I'm talking about everyone in that town who did right by you. Joe. Sarah. John. Emma. All of them. You told me you loved me and let me think we were planning a future together when you knew that couldn't happen. How could you do that?"

He merely shook his head, as if nothing coming out of my mouth was true. Holding out his hand, he pleaded, "We still can, Clare. This doesn't have to change us or what we have together. The only difference is now I'm not some poor guy who doesn't know who he is. That's all. I have millions. I can afford to give you a life you never dreamed of. We can go tonight and start that life. All you have to do is take my hand and say you understand."

I looked down at his outstretched hand in front of me. He'd held me with that hand night after night, gently running his fingers through my hair as I drifted off to sleep.

But now it looked foreign and strange. Who was this man kneeling in front of me in my living room telling me about being rich and giving me some other kind of life? Who was this man who had convinced me he was some handsome amnesiac? Who was Marco? How was I supposed to just suddenly understand someone who lied to an entire town and to the woman he claimed to love? It wasn't like he told some small lie we could get past like being from Wyoming instead of Minnesota. This was huge.

It was too much.

I shook my head and fought back the tears that pricked at the back of my eyes. "You lied to me. You lied to everyone in this town. All those people I listed? They're going to be devastated. You let everyone think they were helping some poor nice guy who'd gotten hurt. For weeks, you walked around town knowing you weren't Matt but Marco. You spent hours with me and never said a word about this for weeks. How could you do that? How could you say you love me?

Everything we are is based on a lie."

Panic flashed in his eyes. "Clare, please. I can make this right. Come with me to LA and you'll see this can work. I promise. I love you. Please."

As I stood to walk upstairs, he didn't stop pleading his case. "Please, Clare. I know none of this makes any sense right now, but if you just come with me to LA I can explain everything to you. Please. I just...please!"

I couldn't look back at him, even as my heart broke with every word he spoke. I couldn't see that face that made no sense to me anymore. I couldn't look at a man I had trusted with so much and see that everything about him and us had been a lie.

By the time I closed my bedroom door, I couldn't keep the tears in anymore. They rolled down my cheeks as I sobbed and collapsed onto the bed. How could this have happened? I knew the answer before the thought fully formed in my head. I knew he would someday remember. I knew and I let myself fall for him because it felt so good.

So good to have someone care. So good to not be alone anymore. So good to love again.

From the bottom of the stairs, he called up, "Clare, please listen to me! This can still work. We can still work. I love you, and I know you love me. Everything else doesn't matter. Just that we love each other. Give me another chance. Please!"

I didn't answer. I didn't know who he was now. Maybe I never had. Stupid Clare. All the signs were there the whole time, and yet, I ignored them all.

Ten minutes later, I heard the front door close behind him and felt like he'd taken part of me with him when he left. He was off to some star-studded life in LA where he could forget about the mess he left behind.

The person who had loved him for the past two months behind.

After an hour of sobbing, I rolled over and saw a call coming in from Emma. I answered the phone, my throat full and my nose stuffed, and said, "So, I guess you've heard?"

"Oh, honey. What happened? I've heard the news, but obviously it doesn't explain everything. So he's remembered he's a movie star now? I thought they contacted that guy's manager and they said he was off somewhere in Europe."

"He's been lying to everyone, Emma. He knew for a few weeks that he was that Marco guy. He never told me. Now he claims he didn't want to go back because he wanted a break from all the parties and women or something."

"Oh my God, Clare. I'm so sorry. Did he come talk to you?"

K . M .   S C O T T

"Yeah. He left about an hour ago. He's probably getting on a flight to LA in Philly by now. He wanted me to go with him. Like it didn't matter that he lied to me about knowing who he really was for weeks. I can't just forgive something like that."

"Oh, honey. I'm sorry. I really thought he was a great guy."

I sniffled and dried my tears before looking over at the side of the bed where he always slept. "But Emma, I really loved him. How could he do this? Why didn't he just tell me when he remembered? I'm not sure it would be much better, but it wouldn't have been worse. God, this is worse than Colin. This is worse than anything I could have ever imagined. Everything was a lie."

"I know you did, Clare, but if he just found out who he really is a few weeks ago, then not everything was a lie."

Emma could always be counted on for seeing the bright side of any situation, but at this moment, I had a hard time believing her. "Two weeks. Three weeks. What does it matter? He lied. All those hours we spent together, and not once did he even mention he was remembering even a tiny bit of his real life. I should have never given him a chance. Damnit, I knew he had amnesia. How did I think this would end up?"

"Don't think of it that way, Clare. You gave

someone a chance. Ever since Colin, you were too afraid to open up to anyone. That's important."

Closing my eyes, I struggled to will the tears away as I remembered how easily Matt had made me believe in love again. "I know you're trying to be nice, Emma, but it feels like all of it was for nothing. I should have never given him a chance."

"Oh, don't say that. Do you want me to come over?"

Even seeing my best friend at that moment didn't sound like something I wanted to do. Everything was still too fresh, too raw. "No, I'm going to go shower. I need to be alone and just process this, okay?"

"Okay. Let me know if you need me. I'm right around the corner any time."

"Thanks, Emma."

After a pause, she said, "I know this hurts like hell, honey, but don't beat yourself up for giving someone a chance. Beat him up for what he did, but don't punish yourself for loving someone again."

I never planned on getting in the shower. It was merely a way to get Emma off the phone. She meant well, as she always did, but the truth was that I did need to be alone. I needed to process finding out Matt was Marco, but even more, I needed to process losing something that meant the world to me.

Instead of holding back my tears, I let them come until I had no more. For hours, I tried to remember if I'd missed any clue that Matt had shown me, any time when he slipped about something while we talked.

But I couldn't think of a single thing. He'd played his part so well, but then again, he was an actor. That's who he was.

Not the man who fixed things at the Colonial Inn and made me smile when no one else could. Not the person I wanted to spend the rest of my life with.

Not Matt.

My father had been right. Love was a lie and a waste of good people's time.

CHAPTER SEVENTEEN

Marco

I T ALWAYS AMAZED me how fast a person could replace one part of the world with another. While Clare remained back in Hansonville, I sat in first class watching the clouds out of the airplane window and wishing more than anything that she was there looking at them beside me. She would have known what kind of clouds they were and would have told me all about them and when I asked how she had all this cloud knowledge, she'd answer some book or some old TV show, her eyes wide with enthusiasm as she happily talked about them. Instead, I sat alone as the inflight movie droned on in the headphones I mainly kept in so no one would speak to me. I wanted to be left alone and get home to start life over.

Again.

I'd done this before. Not the amnesia part. And certainly not the falling in love part. Just the part about walking away from my life. When things got too heavy and I wanted to drown myself in liquor or lose myself in drugs, I always made the choice to leave.

In the past, I'd privately congratulated myself on being better than getting myself all fucked up. It was so easy in LA, after all. Unhappy? Have a drink. Smoke a blunt. Snort a line. Take whatever the fuck you wanted so the unhappy disappeared. That I avoided all that had been a source of pride for me before.

Now I knew running away didn't make me superior. Months of being Matt the handyman at the Colonial Inn in Hansonville proved that. But I had been a better person as him.

When I got off the plane and into the car Sierra had waiting for me, I sat back and closed my eyes. Everything about this place made me want to run. The noise. The busyness. The hurrying.

The driver never tried to speak to me. I stared at that rearview mirror almost the entire ride, but he didn't even glance up to look back at me once. That would never have happened in Hansonville. Not a day went by without someone in town striking up a conversation with me. Perfect strangers smiled at me as they passed, and when I smiled back, something I rarely did back here in LA, they talked. Small talk about the weather or the food at the Patriot or whatever the topic of the day in town was.

It didn't matter. They talked.

When the car came to a stop in my driveway, I sighed and silently got out, but unlike every other time I'd done this, I tapped on the driver's window. I watched as it slowly lowered to reveal a man looking out at me with wide eyes, like he couldn't imagine what I could want. He probably thought I wanted to ream him out for something.

"Thank you for the ride. I appreciate it."

For a moment, he just stared up at me. I'd never said thank you to drivers or anyone else in their position in this town. Finally, he smiled, but I had the sense that it was more to make me go away than anything genuine.

That didn't matter, though. He may not think I should say thank you, but now I knew. After spending all that time in Hansonville, I knew a lot I'd forgotten in my time in LA.

I trudged up my front steps into my house and threw my bag onto the couch. I missed the smell of the trees back in Hansonville. My house smelled like it always had. Like nothing. The place literally had not a single scent to it.

Sterile. Spotlessly clean. Unlived in. That was my home.

Sierra showed up a half hour later. Marching through my front door toward where I stood in the kitchen, she said, "You've given me a headache for months, Marco. But I missed you. How are you?"

I shrugged, utterly disinterested in having this or any other discussion. "Fine. Why are you here?"

"Well, to check on you, of course!"

I knew by how forced her answer sounded that she wasn't being entirely honest. I rolled my eyes and headed toward my room, stripping out of my shirt halfway down the hall. She followed me and stood in my doorway as I considered whether I wanted to go to bed or start drinking.

"Do you have something you need to tell me, Sierra?" I asked after tossing my shirt onto the bed.

She didn't get the chance to answer before I pushed past her and began walking out toward the living room. I had whisky there. Maybe gin. If I had to stay here, I needed to get the bar stocked.

Turning back to look at her as she followed me like a duckling behind its mother, I asked, "You want a drink?"

"A drink? You don't usually drink unless it's at parties, Marco."

"I do now," I answered as I made a beeline for the bar in the corner of the room.

I'd literally never walked behind the thing. Every party I'd had in this house I hired a bartender. Oh well. How hard could it be to toss ice into a glass and fill it up with alcohol? It's not like I needed anything fancy.

Just something that would help me forget.

As I busied myself with getting a drink, Sierra stood staring at me in shock. "How are you?"

"Sierra, are you going to get to the point or not? If I need a therapist, I'll pay for one."

Her shocked expression morphed into a look of hurt for a brief moment before she kicked into work mode. "Fair enough. I heard from the studio, and we need to make some moves before the option runs out. Now nothing has been affected by this stunt of yours, thank God, so I think we need to pull the trigger within the week."

I drank down a glass of whisky. My throat burning, I croaked out, "Fine. Get me the paperwork."

"That's it? You don't have any other questions?"

She set her bag down on the coffee table in front of the black leather sofa. Her high heels clicked sharply and annoyingly across the floor to in front of the bar and stopped. She clearly wasn't getting the hint that I wanted her gone.

"What questions? It's a script. I memorize it. I act it out. I'm not new to this, for fuck's sake, Sierra."

My bluntness caught her off guard, and I watched her mouth drop open. Her presence irritated me. All I knew was I wanted to be alone with enough whisky to get so blasted that I could forget.

"Listen, Marco. I get it. You had this traumatic event and all. I know. But I need to know for sure that if you're signing onto this that you're really in it. I can't have you backing out or losing focus midway through a project like this. Especially since you're on location for three months. Can you do this?"

What else did I have to do? She acted like I had a life full of great things that would make going somewhere difficult.

"Yes."

That's all I said before turning my focus back to pouring myself another drink. I didn't bother with ice on the second one. That would only dilute the whisky and make it harder to get loaded.

Not that I'd have a tough time. All those years proudly staying clean except for social drinking meant by the time I downed three drinks that I'd be passed out.

All the better.

Still Sierra didn't leave. She looked like she was worried that if she did that I might do something to hurt myself. Well, other than starting out on the road to ruining my liver.

"Marco, I'm worried about you."

"Don't be. I'm a grown man. I'll be fine."

That last part was one of the biggest lies I'd ever spoken.

"It's just not like you to stand around shirtless behind your bar drinking liquor like this. Do you want to talk?"

Was she fucking kidding?

"To you or in general?" I asked before tipping the glass up to my mouth to down the last of my second drink. "Because the answer to both is a resounding no."

My words hit her hard, and she winced like they actually hurt. I'd never been this brusque with Sierra. She told me what I needed to do, and I did it. When I jumped from my life each time, she found me and pulled me back.

And round and round my life went. Except this time I didn't know if I could do it. At the moment, I couldn't.

Marching past her back to my room, I grabbed a clean shirt and made my way back out to where she stood waiting for me. Without a word, I spun around and walked toward the door. If I stayed, she'd talk herself into a coma, and I wasn't about to stay around for it. I trusted her in my house. She could enjoy it. I certainly wasn't.

I got in my Maserati and drove down to my

buddy Ollie's house. Unlike Sierra, I wanted to talk to him.

He opened his front door and laughed. "Bro! What the fuck have you been doing with yourself? We need to catch up man. How you been?"

I'd known Ollie since we'd both arrived in LA when we were teenagers. We'd both gotten in good with the right crowd. He'd gone the comedy route while I'd stuck with the dramatic roles. He was goofy but women went crazy for it. He wasn't a bad looking guy either. Tall with dark hair, the magazines described him as the funny guy with a secret. That cracked me up.

I shrugged. "Fine. You guys still haven't gotten yourselves canceled, huh?" I asked, assuming his good mood meant he still had a gig.

"Nah, we got renewed for two more seasons. But between you and me, I'm looking at some movie deals here soon."

"Oh yeah? Moving in on my turf?" I joked.

"Trying. So what's this I hear about you hanging out incognito in Pennsylvania?"

"Oh yeah, sorry, man."

"Sorry? What the fuck for? It's brilliant. I hear everyone was going crazy for it. Broody Marco Randolph off lost in the woods. That shit sells, man. You'll be a straight to cable movie in no time. Not cool what the stand in did, though. The guy knew his job and he put you at risk. Not okay."

I chuckled at his busting my ass. "Fuck you. But thanks."

"Well, come in and tell me what life in small-town America is like. Did you have fun?"

Suddenly, I didn't want to talk to anyone, even Ollie. I didn't want to try to explain how living in Hansonville made me see things differently. He may have understood, but it didn't matter. Everything I loved back there was gone now. Talking about it wasn't going to make it come back.

"Nah, I have to go, but I wanted to check in and say I'm still alive. You know me. I always come back, right?"

Ollie looked around at his enormous front yard and smiled. "Who the hell wouldn't want to come back to this? But I get needing to check out every so often. It's an occupational hazard. Hit me up when you're in the mood to go out. I could use a night out like the old days."

As I smiled and lied about looking forward to that, I wondered if he'd ever thought of giving it all up for anyone. Who knew? Maybe there was a Clare in Ollie's past somewhere.

FOR AN HOUR, I drove around Hollywood Hills as the sun started to set. Not a single fucking soul seemed to be even bothered that I'd checked out of my life once again without a thought about anyone but myself. Even Sierra only seemed inconvenienced. Now that I was back and about to make a boatload of money again, she was fine. Ollie wasn't pissed. He may not even have noticed I disappeared until recently.

Then again, I supposed it didn't seem all that surprising to me, after all. I mean, what Ollie said was right. I hadn't done anything wrong. The guy trying to buy sex on the street who was supposed to be me was the bad guy.

When I got back to my place, Sierra was nowhere to be found. She'd left a note on the counter with a smiley face drawn under the words, "Good to have you back."

Within a couple days, my life went back to what it had always been. I messaged Ollie and for the rest of the week we partied like we had before we had careers to jeopardize. His divorce had wrapped up a few months before I'd left, so we were knee deep in women and booze.

My place became party central, and one night I found myself drunk off my ass, standing in the middle of my Hollywood castle. I looked around my kingdom and it was a sea of legs and tits and dresses that barely covered either. Ollie and a few other friends raised their glasses at me and I repeated the motion.

To everyone around me, life had returned to

what it was supposed to be. For me, though, I never stopped thinking of Clare.

I didn't even know most of the people at this party. There was always a group of willing young women who wanted a night with the stars. Some would get fucked, and the ones who didn't would tell everyone they had. I couldn't even remember some of the names of the guys Ollie brought with him, as if there was some kind of obligatory dude to chick ratio that had to be maintained. I didn't care.

That was just this life. Fast cars, easy women, and more alcohol than I knew what to do with. At least that was what it was supposed to be.

Ollie raised his glass and called out, "To the coolest fucking guy in this town! Such a good actor a bunch of hicks didn't even know who he was for months!"

Everyone raised their glasses and toasted me. I smiled and tossed back my drink. Funny how things went back to normal faster than even I had thought they would.

One of the guys standing next to me leaned over and said, "We were just talking about that. That stand-in is an ass. Putting you at risk like that? Nah. Nah, bro. Not cool."

I gave him a sympathetic smile, like I cared what he thought, and looked around for the bottle of whisky. After pouring myself another glass and taking a gulp, from behind me I felt a pair of hands slide down my shoulders onto my pecs.

"Hey, baby. Want to party?" a sensual voice whispered in my ear before I felt a small nip on my earlobe.

I looked back and saw it wasn't one of the usual LA party whores Ollie liked to hang out with. No, this woman was stunning. Long blond hair, piercing blue eyes, legs that went on forever and tits big enough for three men to enjoy.

A quick glance at Ollie and he smirked. "It's only right you get the hottest girl here. It is your house."

I rolled my eyes and walked off with the woman. She might've said her name. I didn't know. I didn't care. She wasn't someone I planned to spend a lot of time with. On our way to the bedroom, she grabbed three of her friends to join us.

I'd been crashing on my couch in a drunken stupor since being back, so my bedroom looked pristine. The three women sat themselves in a line at the end of my bed as the blonde stood behind me, rubbing my shoulders.

"So, which one strikes your fancy?"

I looked at the line of beautiful women in front of me sitting on my black bedspread. Two blondes and a redhead, they were stunning, but they weren't what I wanted deep down and even through the alcohol a part of me knew that. I walked over and sat in a large chair near my dresser and looked at all of them once more before shrugging.

"Why don't you girls just amuse yourselves?" I said, already bored and wishing I'd filled up my glass before we came back here.

They began to kiss one another as the stunning woman walked over and sat in my lap. I sighed and shook my head. Looking past her, I saw Ollie walk by my bedroom door and give me big thumbs up and a wink before he trailed off with a group of women of his own.

Rolling my eyes at this whole fucking business, I looked at the woman pawing at my pants and said, "Don't you want more than this?

She looked at me quizzically and shook her head. "What more is there? Did you make it big to not fuck beautiful women and drink until you black out?"

"No."

"Then why did you do it?"

"I…I don't know," I said.

It was the most honest thing I'd uttered since returning to LA. She stared at me for another moment and I looked into her eyes. I wanted to see Clare in there somewhere. I wanted to see a woman who wanted beautiful things in the world and not just to fuck movie stars who were more famous than her.

But I saw nothing there. Nothing at all.

I let her stay on my lap a while, pawing at me, knowing if I didn't then all the sites the next day would be talking about how I'd changed and how my entire career could be in crisis. Bullshit stuff but press I didn't need at the moment.

Every time I thought of that fucking stand-in and what he did, I hated him more. Thanks to him, everything had come crashing down, and instead of letting Clare know the truth in my own time, I'd been forced to have it happen the way it had.

The women on the bed continued to give me a show and after a while they were either too drunk or too tired to continue. One by one, I eased them out of my room, assuring them all that they'd been wonderful. They'd all lie and say they'd slept with me, even though they hadn't. If they told people the truth, they'd worry not that the question would be about my sexuality, but their ability to arouse me. It was a crazy town we lived in.

The actress, whose name I'd actively forgotten while she'd told me it, stayed the longest but finally walked out as she said, "Baby, people in this town, they either sink or they swim. You look like you're sinking, Marco Randolph."

She left me alone, and I sat down on my bed, irritated that some bimbo who probably starred on CSI Boise thought she knew anything about me. Fuck her.

I didn't give a damn about her or anyone else. I knew what I needed to do, so I dialed the numbers and waited.

She answered, and just hearing her voice sent my heart soaring. "Hello?"

"Clare, it's me. Marco."

She hung up instantly. I kept the phone to my ear even though there was no sound coming from hers. Just hearing her say that single word had been the best thing in days.

I mustered up the courage to call her again, but when she answered instead of saying hello she said, "I don't want to talk to you. Not now. Not ever. Do not call me."

She ended the call a second time, and I knew if I kept trying it would do no good. I couldn't give up, though. I just needed to find a way to make her see we could work.

Then an idea came to me. I dialed the number of the person I knew could talk to Clare and who probably didn't hate me.

"Hello?" she said hesitantly.

"Emma. It's me, Marco. Or, well, Matt."

"Marco, hi. Why are you calling me?"

My heart racing, I took a deep breath and let

it out slowly. "I know this is kind of a long shot, but I was hoping you could talk to Clare for me."

"I don't know. She's really hurt, Marco."

"I know. I never meant for that to happen. If I could just get her to hear me out…"

My sentence trailed off to silence since I didn't know what would happen if she did. Maybe she'd still tell me to fuck off. I didn't want to think about that right now, though.

"Can I ask you a question?" Emma said quietly.

"I guess. What?"

"Why? Why did you do it? I told you what she went through with the last guy, and still you lied."

And I hated myself for that.

"I'm sorry, Emma. I needed to get away and then after those two guys jumped me, I didn't know who I was. That wasn't a lie. When I did remember who I was, I didn't know how to tell her and still have to be the person I am here. I never meant to lie. I just didn't want to lose her. What I had with Clare, what I felt for her, that wasn't a lie, though. It never was. Please Emma, will you talk to her for me? Will you try to get her to come around? I can give her an amazing life if she'd just forgive me."

She didn't speak for a long time but finally said, "I guess I can try, but I can't promise anything. Sometimes it's just too much and it can't be fixed."

"Thank you, Emma."

I didn't want to believe what happened between Clare and me couldn't be fixed. The love we had was real. In a city where that couldn't be said for many things, I knew real when I found it.

Clare just had to give me another chance. We could be happy again if she did.

That's all I needed. Another chance.

CHAPTER EIGHTEEN

Clare

F OR NEARLY A week, I hid out in my house, unable to face the people in town. They'd always thought of me as odd. I imagined they now thought of me as pathetic.

Strange girl or sad girl. Those were my choices.

My boss allowed me to take an emergency vacation, even though that left the office with only one person and she was practically brand new at the job. Normally, I'd care about that, but this time I just couldn't.

Each day, I woke up and drifted from my bed to the shower with no discernable reason for why I needed to. Hermits didn't exactly need to smell good or even look presentable. I ordered delivery from the only two places in town that offered it. I wouldn't go out. I didn't want to be seen by anyone or go to the places Matt and I had frequented and be reminded of him and all his lies.

Marco. I had to stop thinking of him as Matt. That's not who he was or who he had ever been. We all knew the truth now.

On day five, I sat down on my bed near lunchtime and the tears overtook me again. It wasn't only that he'd lied. That was simply a portion of the pain. Where the real hurt came from was that I'd let myself believe in love again. I'd let myself think that this time the handsome stranger who came to town wouldn't hurt me. Why was I always so stupid?

I walked downstairs and the numbness didn't go anywhere but instead made a home inside my heart and mind. That was the only protection I had from all the pain. If I could wall myself up and not let the world in, maybe I could avoid how much this hurt.

Had it all been my fault? Had I been so stupid that I hadn't recognized a movie star right in front of my eyes? No one that good looking just showed up in a small town like Hansonville. Had I'd just been naive and blind to the truth that had been right in front of me for so long?

I sighed and glanced into my living room as I walked toward my kitchen. I hadn't yet been able to spend more than a minute in that room since the day I learned that the last few months of my life and the love I'd come to believe in had all been a lie. Now, though, another memory shot through my mind, one of that same living room but made even more painful by the most recent events.

My father sat in his recliner, his gray hair shining in the sunlight that poured through the big front window. Ready to go out with some friends, I rushed down the stairs and stopped when he called my name.

"Clare, come on in here. I want to talk to you"

I stopped, irritated that if I didn't leave at that moment I'd be late. "What's up, Dad?" I asked, fidgeting with my purse as I wished to leave our depressing house and into the world with my friends to go to Philadelphia.

He looked up from the television and asked, "Are you seeing that boy Jacob today?"

"I think he's coming with the group, but I'm not sure."

I'd made the mistake a few weeks earlier of telling my father that I liked a boy and that he seemed to like me too. Things were moving glacially slow between us, but my father refused to hear any of it. He was livid that I wanted to date.

The lectures about love not being real and the people you love deceiving you then began in earnest. Every day, he mentioned it, as if I could ever forget after all I'd seen happen to him because of my mother.

My father sat back, his blue eyes sad, and said, "I want you to be careful, Clare."

"I always am, Daddy."

"You know what I mean. Boys will tell you anything to get to you. It doesn't matter if they want what's under your skirt or your heart. They'll lie to get either one."

"Jeez, dad! I get it. Just stop worrying about me, okay?"

He shook his head and frowned. "I can't do that. I'm your father." Reaching into his pocket, he pulled out a couple twenties. "Here, take this and have a good time in Philly today."

"Dad, what? I…how did you know?"

One of his rare smiles lit up his face. "I work with Emma's mother, Clare. Parents talk. Just have fun and don't forget what I told you. Don't let any boy get too close. Love isn't worth it."

That was my father. Angry at the world and terrified of it but sweet to me. He couldn't help it. I was the only person who'd ever loved him for real.

I stood there staring into the living room I couldn't stand to be in now, and I could hear my father warning me plain as day. The weight of just how right he had been settled all around me.

The next day I woke up to the sound of someone banging on my door. I put on my robe and walked down the stairs to open it and saw Emma standing there on my porch. It disgusted me to admit that a small part of me had wondered if it might be him.

"You haven't been answering your phone. So I took the day off and I'm spending it with you. You don't get to say no or that you're fine. Nope. So open up, Clare. You're getting a best friend day."

"Thanks, Emma, but I don't know," I said.

Emma sighed. "You can't go on like this forever. It's my job as your friend to tell you that."

"Why? Why can't I just accept this is my life?"

She shook her head and smiled. "Because it isn't. Now let me in, or I'm going to knock you over."

I stepped out of the way as she walked in. "Since I'm not in any shape to defend myself, I guess I have no choice."

Turning back to face me, she said, "No, I guess you don't. So how are you holding up? You look like warmed over shit, but that's because you've been holed up in this house all week."

"You didn't mention this was a tough love visit."

Emma shrugged and gave me a gentle smile. "Sorry, but it is. Now tell me the truth. How are you?"

"You want the truth? Okay. Not great. I've

been thinking about how right my father was about everything, and I feel like a damned fool. I never should have let him in."

"Listen, I loved your father, but that garbage about never falling in love was crap. Sorry. As for feeling like a fool, don't you dare. You did nothing wrong, so you shouldn't take any of the blame."

I huffed my disgust at that and my own idiocy. "I fell in love with a man who had amnesia, Emma. I should have known it would turn out bad."

She took a deep breath and blew the air out of her lungs in a rush. "Well, some of that is true, but you let someone in and fell in love. That's a good thing, no matter how bad you feel. And he loved you. He did and you know it, so don't bother arguing with me about that fact."

Rolling my eyes at her defense of me, I said, "Fine, I won't argue. But you can't argue that he lied about who he was for weeks instead of telling me the truth."

"Point taken."

We stood there silent for a few moments before she said, "So, everyone in town officially knows now, but I guess you already knew that."

"I'd assumed."

"No one is even that mad at him, honestly. It's such a crazy story. I know that's not how you think of it, but to everyone on the outside of things, it just seems like some sort of random gossip. Stuff like that doesn't happen in Hansonville."

"No one is mad?" I asked, astonished.

How could people not be mad at him after he betrayed everyone? I hadn't expected the whole town to show up in my name with torches and pitchforks, but to hear that no one was mad at him floored me.

"Not really, no. John is thrilled that he gets to tell everyone he gave a beat-up truck to a movie star. And the Patriot is using the fact that he ate there in their new advertising. It sure didn't take them long to get that together."

I sighed in disbelief. "I can't believe no one is mad at him. Leave it to Hansonville to get so caught up in one movie star and forget he lied to them and used them like props for weeks."

Emma frowned and walked away into the kitchen. I followed her and found her standing next to my refrigerator pouring herself a glass of iced tea. "I know he hurt you, but everyone else didn't know him like you did."

"I didn't know him at all. Everything was an act by a clearly gifted actor. Even someone as cynical about love as me couldn't see through his bullshit. What my father always said was right. I should have listened."

"Have you talked to him at all?"

I looked at her in shock. How could she ask that? "Talked to him? Jesus, no. I can't talk to him."

"I see. Has he tried to call you?"

"Yes, why?"

"Well, he called me," she said in her hopeful tone, as if him calling her to get to me was anywhere in the realm of okay.

I raised my eyebrows in surprise. "Why would he be calling you? What, is he looking for a new woman to lie to? I wouldn't suggest diving in. Movie star or not, they all end up breaking your heart."

"You sound like your dad."

"Three guesses why."

I was being bratty. I knew that deep down. But I felt justified in my brattiness to a degree.

When Emma didn't continue talking, I couldn't stop myself from asking, "You said he called you?"

"Yeah. He did. He's really broken up about the whole thing, Clare. He sounded like he was a wreck."

"And that's supposed to convince me to forgive him?"

"No. But he begged me for my help. He loves you, and he's sorry."

"I'm not listening to this." I said as I began

pacing across my kitchen.

"Do you remember how he came to me and asked for help for his date with you? How he stomached that macaroni and cheese even though he hated it? That all seemed pretty real to me."

"Actor. They routinely do things like that while they're acting. Some of them lose tons of weight for a role. I don't think eating a few forkfuls of macaroni and cheese shows he cared for me."

I couldn't listen to any more of this. Maybe Emma didn't deserve the full brunt of my anger, but it was barreling her way from the start of the conversation and I certainly couldn't stop it when she mentioned that stuff about our first few dates.

Marching past her, I opened my mouth to tell her to stop when she added, "Maybe you should focus on the positive things that were actually real about him, Clare."

That was it. I stopped walking and turned to face her. "Are you kidding me? Are you seriously defending him right now?"

"No! Clare, that's not what I meant. I'm sorry."

Deep down inside, I knew Emma was only trying to help, but I shouldn't be getting a talking to about looking at the positive side of things. She was forgetting that I had done that and look where it had gotten me.

"Listen, Emma. I appreciate you coming over here and all. I really do. But this isn't some average breakup. This is something seriously messed up that's happened. Maybe you and everyone else in this town are fine with the fact that a man repeatedly lied to your face and used you all, but I'm not okay with it. I'm not just going to focus on the positive and get over it."

She began to speak, but I needed to get out my hurt, one way or another. I held my hand up and stopped her.

"It's not okay. Someone needs to hold him responsible for the damage he caused. And maybe I'm being selfish and hateful. Maybe I'm being like my father. But he hasn't been wrong so far. So thank you for coming, but I need to be alone right now. I can't take hearing someone tell me that they've been getting desperate calls from my ex for them to come over and try to patch things up between us. This isn't high school, Emma. This is real, and I am really freaking hurt thanks to that guy you're defending."

Emma's shoulders sagged from all I'd just said to her. As she made her way toward the living room to leave, she turned around to look back at me. "Listen, I know you're hurt right now. I'm sorry. I really am. But I'm around whenever you need me. Okay?"

"Okay," I answered, unable to look at her.

I heard her sigh, but she didn't say anything more before she turned around and walked to the front door. I didn't care if the entire world thought Marco Randolph wasn't the villain in our little play. They could forgive him for lying, but I couldn't.

Not now. Not ever.

CHAPTER NINETEEN

Marco

TWO WEEKS HAD passed since Hansonville. Since Clare. I'd partied as hard as I could to try and forget everything. For a few moments, I had even begun to believe that it would all be fine. It hadn't been my fault. I was just misunderstood.

But something about the way that no one else made me feel bad for what I did, not even the media, left me as the only one who would do it. It took a while, but I did. I sat in my huge house, surrounded by things to share with someone that didn't exist for me anymore, and slumped down on my couch.

When the party faded was always when I felt the lowest. This time, though, the party ended with a whole lot more on my shoulders than just being alone again. Without anyone else to fill the void, my house felt massive and lonely.

From a few rooms away, I heard my phone go off. I raced to it, hoping it would be Clare calling to give me a second chance. Unlikely, but I couldn't give up hope.

I got to my cell and saw that hope in the form of a familiar number. "Emma! How are you?"

"Fine, Marco. So, listen, I talked to Clare and she wouldn't hear anything nice about you. I think I pushed a little too hard. She asked me to leave and that's never happened in all the time I've known her."

I sighed as disappointment made me feel like I had a hundred pound weight on my shoulders. Now I'd ruined her relationship with Clare too. "I'm sorry, Emma. I'm sure she'll come around."

"To me? Yeah, our friendship will survive one spat. But listen, Marco. It's over. She doesn't want to hear about you, never mind from you. I'm sorry."

"I appreciate you trying, Emma. Thanks."

She ended the call without a goodbye, leaving me standing in that damned empty house again.

"Fuck!"

There had to be a way to fix this. I had to figure out how to get Clare to talk to me again. If she would just listen and hear me out.

As I stewed in my own misery trying to come up with some way to get her back, I suddenly thought of something that might work.

Had to work.

I grabbed my phone and quickly called Sierra.

"Hello? Marco? Why are you calling me at seven in the morning on a Wednesday? You know I'm more of a nine a.m. kind of girl, right?"

"Sierra, I know. Listen, I need your help."

"With what?"

I didn't answer immediately, and she quickly asked, "Does this have to do with the woman you left in that tiny town, Marco?"

"Does it matter? I need your help with something that won't hurt my career, so are you going to help me?"

Of course, the mention of anything relating to money piqued her interest. "What is it?"

"Who is the biggest name in bluegrass right now?"

"Seriously? Like I would know. Bluegrass? I'm assuming some dad band from Nebraska. Why?"

"Sierra, focus. I need you to find me the biggest name in bluegrass. I don't care how much they cost. I need them to do a concert for me in Hansonville, Pennsylvania on Saturday."

"Marco, I don't know if that's possible."

"Are you the best in this town like you claim to be?" I asked, knowing if I involved her pride in the mix there would be no turning back for her.

She chuckled and said, "Okay, but even people in the business get to sleep until eight, Marco. I'll call you this afternoon when I have more information."

"Thank you. I'll have more info for you later too. I need this done perfectly, Sierra."

"Nothing but the best for you."

I barely put the phone down before my fingers were flying across the keys of my laptop. Sierra would handle the band, but I needed to set up things with the venue personally. If Clare was going to believe I was truly sorry, she needed to know I would speak with the people in Hansonville myself.

Fighting back nerves at how Sarah would react to hearing me on the other end of the phone, I called the Colonial Inn. She answered in her usual friendly voice and when I told her it was me, I could practically hear her smile broaden.

"Matt! I'm so happy to hear from you. But I guess it's not Matt, right? You'll always be Matt Doe to me, though. How have you been, hon?"

"I'm okay, but before I tell you what I'm calling about, I want to tell you how sorry I am for lying. I never meant to hurt you or Joe or anyone in town. I just didn't want it all to end."

"Oh, honey. I get it. Everyone thinks being a famous movie star would be a dream come true, but you found real happiness here. I know that. And you don't have to apologize. We all sort of feel like we got to be bit players in your movie you acted out right here, so not another word about being sorry."

Relieved she and Joe didn't hate me, I took a deep breath and set about telling her what I wanted to do. When I finished explaining my idea, she squealed, "I love this! What do you want to call it?"

"What do you mean? Whoever the band ends up being. I'll know that later on today or tomorrow."

"We need something for the advertisements. You want everyone in town there, right? How about Celebrity Marco Randolph: An Apology Concert?"

I rolled my eyes so hard I thought I would go into another dimension. "Uh, no. I don't want my name associated with this, Sarah. I want the focus on promoting the band and that it's an impromptu concert for everyone in Hansonville."

"Ooooh, how about Bluegrass in the Tall Grass. You know, because you want to hold it out in that field on the edge of town?"

Leave it to Sarah to come up with something cute like that. "That works. I'll be in touch with the name of the band. My manager may be the one who calls you, actually. Her name is Sierra."

"That's such a beautiful name. I bet she's gorgeous like everyone is out there," Sarah said in a faraway voice.

"She's great, but I'm hoping this works to convince another beautiful woman to talk to me."

I stopped for a moment and then asked, "Have you seen her? How does she look after…"

I didn't bother finishing my sentence. After she found out I lied wasn't something I wanted to keep reminding everyone about.

"No, I haven't, honey. She hasn't been to work, and I don't think she's come into town since everyone found out."

That bit of news didn't make this any better, but I couldn't focus on that. She'd hear about the bluegrass concert and come into town. I knew she would. Then I could talk to her and fix everything I'd screwed up.

"Okay, Sarah. Well, let everyone there know about Saturday, and I'll see you soon."

Tossing my phone off to the side, I thought about how much I couldn't wait to see Clare in a few days. The image of her flitted through my mind, and how much I truly missed her made my chest ache. The way that little strand of hair would fall in her face, or how she held most of her laugh in unless she really found something funny. I missed all the little things about her. I had to make this grand gesture count.

At around nine that night, Sierra opened my front door and I looked up from my laptop surprised to see her there. "What is it with the house calls recently?"

"I was in the neighborhood. You're not my

only client, you know."

"So? The band?"

"I've got it all set up. And don't worry about anything else, Marco. It's all been handled from here on out. The tents, the alcohol, everything is being taken care of."

Thrilled, I walked over to her and gave her a hug. "Great, I don't want my name near this." I knew how she felt about publicity, but that's not what this was about.

"Well, it won't be advertised that way, according to that nice lady Sarah I spoke to. People will figure out it's you who set it all up, though. They aren't simpletons, Marco. Do you really think this will work?"

"It has to. It's my last try."

"Okay. Before you go rushing off back to that town, I need you to sign some more paperwork for this movie."

"Fine. I'll sign whatever. Just talk to me about all that crap after Saturday. Are you coming to the show?"

Sierra chuckled and threw her expensive purse over her shoulder as she shook her head. "As much as I would just love to meet the woman who has made this change in you, I wouldn't be caught dead in some Podunk town in Pennsylvania."

"Aren't you from a Podunk town in Illinois?"

"I am. And that's why I have a thorough distaste for them. Most of us don't come to LA with big dreams of living in a three bedroom in Illinois."

"Fair enough. How many bedrooms do you have here?"

Sierra twisted her mouth into a frown. "Less than you, Marco. So let's make this movie a hit and I can get more. We'll talk soon. I'll have your flight bookings sent to you tomorrow."

She spun on her heels, making her blond hair twirl around her head, and headed out my front door. For the first time in weeks, a smile crept onto my face. My plan would work out. Clare would see how much I missed her and would want me back. Everyone would see.

A COUPLE DAYS later, I stepped back onto Main Street in Hansonville a few hours before the concert began. After practically getting a hero's welcome from Sarah and Joe at the inn, I hoped that good feeling would extend to everyone else in town, especially Clare.

I crossed the street to head to the Patriot, and before I got inside, I heard a man yell toward me, "Hey, Matt! Good to see you!"

Roger from the grocery store seemed happy to see me. The woman with him called out, "He means Marco! Nice to see you back so soon!"

Over and over, this kind of reunion happened with the citizens of Hansonville, and to a person, they all showered me with adoration. Some wanted pictures taken with me, while others wanted to know if I'd been secretly scouting out locations for some future movie. Not a single one of them even bothered to ask why I'd lied to them for weeks about who I was.

But I knew winning over Clare wouldn't be that easy.

The band Sierra found had just won a Grammy a year ago. To say it was a miracle that they'd agreed to play such a small venue on such short notice was an understatement. Luckily, Ollie's cousin knew the banjo player, of all people, and put in a good word for me and my cause.

By evening time, everyone in town gathered in the empty field near the edge of town and waited for the band to start the show. I'd paid for everyone to have as much food and drinks as they wanted, bringing in dozens of food trucks to add to the Patriot's offerings and more beer than Hansonville had ever seen in its over two hundred year existence.

I hung out behind one of the trucks, smiling for photos with people who approached me but not seeking out any attention. Scanning the area over and over again, I kept trying to find her, but she wasn't there.

"Sweet deal with all this food and drink. Hansonville is going to be hungover tomorrow. I can tell you that much," a familiar voice said behind me.

I turned around to see Emma with a cup of beer in her hand. Raising it, she added, "You sure do know how to put on a party, Mr. Hollywood."

"Well, tomorrow's Sunday, so there are worse days for it," I said with a smile.

I didn't want to jump right to the question that was burning in my mind, but I had to know. Was Clare there with her?

"Marco, I know you wanted this to work, but she refused to come. She's having none of it. Maybe everyone else in this town is willing to forgive you, but she isn't."

"But why? Can't she tell that I obviously love her?"

"It's like I told you. It all goes back to her mom and dad. Everything you did only proved to her that her dad had always been right and that she should have listened to him."

"It's not like that, though."

"I know you don't want to believe that, but it's her history. I'm sorry. I had high hopes for the handsome amnesiac and the beautiful small-town girl."

Disappointed, I looked away at the throngs of people having a good time. "Thanks again for your help, Emma. I really appreciate it."

"Anytime. Hey, can I get an autograph? Turns out my niece loves you and she'll have my head if I don't come home with one."

"Sure. You want a picture for her too?"

"Perfect."

We snapped the picture and I signed the back of a poster with a personalized message to her niece. I handed it all back to Emma and said, "I'm going to go find somewhere quiet. It was nice seeing you, Emma. Enjoy the show."

"Somewhere quiet or Clare's place?"

I shook my head in defeat. "I wouldn't go there. I get it now."

Alone, I took out my cell phone and gave it one last try with Clare. It rang and rang before I hung up. Then I caved and called a second time. Still no answer.

She wouldn't even answer my call, and there was no way she didn't know I was in town. So much for my grand plan.

CHAPTER TWENTY

Clare

I'D HEARD THROUGH my boss about Marco coming to town. I knew what he was doing and didn't like it. I didn't like that Emma called and tried to convince me to go.

He must have thought he was pretty clever getting the best bluegrass band around. But clever didn't mean honest or loving. Clever meant sneaky. I wasn't a fan of sneaky. So I decided not to go.

While a caravan of trucks drove down my road on their way to town, I sat on my front porch and watched them. Then I watched as a limo rolled down the road. A limo he probably sat in.

Still I wanted nothing to do with any of it. He could play his little game with the rest of the town. I'd had enough of Marco Randolph for one lifetime.

When it was nearly time for the show to start,

I walked inside and turned the television on to see the local news airing an interview with Marco. God, these people couldn't get enough of this guy! No wonder he thought this whole stunt would work.

The tiny brunette woman who usually sat at the news desk stood dwarfed by his over six foot height and gazed up at him as she asked, "Marco, can you tell us why you're doing this?"

"I just wanted to show my appreciation for a great town. Hansonville was good to me, so I wanted to repay that."

I rolled my eyes at his newest lie. Why did anyone around here believe a word he said?

"There you have it, folks. Hansonville is the place to be this evening. High River Billies will be playing late into the night here. Come on down and have a free drink thanks to Marco Randolph!"

The camera scanned the crowd, and everyone I knew from the time I was a child was there. Maybe I could go. I loved the band, and the whole town had turned out. I thought about going upstairs and getting dressed for the first time in days, but I didn't have anything to wear to something like this anyway.

But I knew that wasn't the real issue keeping me away. No matter how much I wanted to see the band, I couldn't bear to face the whole town at once. Everyone knew what happened to me. It didn't matter if the town forgave him like Emma said they did. They'd still look at me with that expression of pity I'd seen on their faces after Colin left. I was only human, and I couldn't bear to face the humiliation.

As much as I dreaded that, I found myself driving into town a half hour later. Maybe I would just sit in my car with the window down and enjoy some music on my own without the rest of the damned town needing to know about it.

When I pulled up, I couldn't believe the size of the crowd. I saw my boss walk by, Emma, the waitress from the Patriot, everyone was there. I pulled out my phone to text Emma and tell her I'd decided to come after all but saw that Marco had called me and stopped dead.

Should I call him back? I hesitated and then the music started. I had to admit the band sounded amazing. I thought about that night, the first night, when we went to Jasper's. Most guys were awkward about dancing. They'd oblige their wives sometimes but only because they felt guilty or indebted.

Had that night been a lie? When we were dancing and smiling and he said he had a good time, had that all been a lie? It couldn't have been. He said it wasn't.

Shaking my head, I looked at my reflection in

the rear view mirror. What was I doing? Was I really thinking I loved him too?

I got out of my car and stood there as a sea of people danced while the band played, and no one singled me out. No one called out, "Hey, there's that woman Marco fooled!" In fact, no one noticed me at all.

Just then I saw him rushing out to the limo parked on Main Street. He seemed to give the place one final glance before getting into the back seat. Was he leaving so early?

That's when it hit me. I loved him. I hated the lies. I hated that he'd misled me, but I loved him. Looking around at the event he'd put together for me, I saw he loved me to.

He couldn't leave yet! I ran back to my car and took off following the limo. I knew it would be a long shot, but if I could catch it before it hit the last stop light in town, maybe I could stop him. I grabbed my phone and called his number, but he didn't answer.

Maybe my not showing up had shown him I didn't care. I called and called again, but he never answered. Ironically enough, it was right near where they'd found him on the highway that I lost the limo ahead of me for good.

I turned the car around and made my way to my house. I was haphazardly throwing things in a suitcase to follow him when I heard the woman on the news say, "The star of the night may have left to go shoot his new movie, but the party rages on! Come on down to Hansonville and have yourself a good time!"

Marco left to shoot a movie? Where?

It wasn't hard to find a report online about his next film and how he'd be on location for the next few months. As the words flowed before my eyes, I slumped in my chair. It was over. I'd had a chance to forgive him and missed it. He'd be in Brazil for the next three months and probably all cuddled up with some Brazilian beauty to boot. It was too much.

I dissolved into tears there in my living room, my half-packed bag in front of me. I hadn't been wrong about being mad. I knew that. I could've shown up at the bluegrass show, though. I could've heard him out when he asked me to. I could've done a lot of things differently that wouldn't have left me sobbing as the love of my life left Hansonville for good.

Three hours later, I was still in tears. Three days later, I felt good enough to smile when I heard his name at work. Three weeks later and I still wasn't over Marco. I thought that in nearly a month's time my feelings would have faded, but they'd only intensified. I tried getting in touch with his manager, but she never returned any of my calls.

So I gave up and returned to my normal life in good old Hansonville.

No one really chose to speak to me too much about it. My boss, a kind man in his late fifties, made a remark about how some men were just thick in the head like a bull in the ass. That cheered me up for a few minutes, but that could be said about me too.

I ate lunch at the Patriot and no one said anything to me about it directly, but I suspected they all wanted to know. They asked me how I'd been, how things were looking for me, the normal things people asked in casual conversations with relative strangers, but nothing direct. I probably would've preferred the directness, but I knew they were trying to be decent and polite people. I couldn't fault them for that. Life moved on for everyone, and only Emma knew how hurt I really was.

Five weeks later and I still missed him. I went through the motions of life, but none of it felt real now. One evening after work, I sat on the couch watching one of those entertainment specials I'd become more interested in since Marco left. Somehow it felt like I was part of that world with him as I watched them every night.

"You know, for someone who doesn't miss him and doesn't love him, you sure do seem to like to watch these shows that gossip about movie stars," Emma said with a smile.

"I'm not dignifying that comment with one of my own," I joked, hoping to hear some tidbit about Marco and silently praying to God it wouldn't include how he'd fallen in love with some gorgeous Brazilian model while on location.

Even before the host launched into the story about him, I saw his picture on the screen. Tanned from the Brazilian sun, he looked incredible. And happy. I knew that should make me happy, but all I felt was a pain in the pit of my stomach.

He'd moved on. Even worse, I had no one to blame but myself.

The interviewer asked him a couple questions about the movie he was working on before saying, "One of the big motivations for your character is his regret. What's your biggest regret, Marco?"

He looked away from the interviewer and straight into the camera and said, "Clare. I miss you, and even if you've forgotten about me, I haven't forgotten about you."

The interviewer wrapped things up and I looked over at Emma as tears filled my eyes.

"Do you want to talk about it?"

"I miss him, Emma. I was wrong to let him go. I knew that the night of the concert and I've known it ever since. He lied, and that's never going to be okay, but I love him all the same and I forgive him."

She smiled and held up her phone. "You know who you should be saying all of that to?"

"I know, I know. But I can't!"

"Why the hell not?"

"I've tried calling the number he called me from, but it's been disconnected since the day after the concert."

Emma smiled and pulled a card out of her purse. "That's because he's on another continent, silly. Here. He gave me this the night of the concert. I think he didn't want you to throw it away or he would have given it to you."

"That's fair," I said, nodding. "I probably would have. Well, I'm going to call him!"

"Okay, but I want to listen!" Emma said, making me feel like we were right back in high school.

I nodded and dialed the strange number, all the while my hands shaking. The phone line rang and rang, but no one answered. Finally, I heard his voice, but it was just the introduction to his voicemail.

"You've reached Marco Randolph. Leave your name and I'll get back to you." Beep.

There in that silence after the beep I froze. I hadn't rehearsed what I wanted to say. Beside me, Emma flailed her hands to egg me on, but my mind went blank.

Finally, I said, "Marco, it's Clare. I miss you too and I've never forgotten you for a second. I love you."

I pressed the red button on my phone and looked over at Emma. "I got his voicemail. Now all I can do is hope he hears it."

She hugged me for a second and pulling back said, "You deserve this, Clare. Okay? You do. You deserve romance and wonder and handsome movie stars who have good looking friends for your best friend."

"Emma, I don't know if we're going to get back together. I don't know anything and I refuse to get my hopes up again until he calls."

"Okay, but when everything works out you remember who was here and single."

Thank God for Emma. My best friend made me laugh when I felt like I might burst into tears again. As she chattered on about movie stars and silly things like that, I couldn't help but wonder. What if he never got the voicemail? Should I call back? Would that look desperate?

Even more, when was that interview done? It didn't seem live, so maybe it happened weeks ago and he'd moved on since.

And if we did actually reunite, logistically, how could we even be together? Did I want to move to LA and just be the girlfriend of some movie star? Was that who I was? I loved my hometown, even though it didn't seem that way a lot of times.

Shaking myself out of my daydreaming, I smiled at Emma, who already had herself set up with some guy Marco knew named Ollie. I needed to stop putting the cart in front of the horse. Marco may never call me back. He may have met someone. He might have given up on us.

When I crawled into bed that night, I wanted to be positive and believe in us, but my thoughts became plagued with doubts. Marco was a handsome guy and a wealthy movie star. Why would he want to hold onto some small-town girl like me? I'd seen his costar in his latest movie, the one being filmed in Brazil. She was stunning in a way that I could never compare to. She was stunning in the same way all the women who surrounded movie stars always were.

So why would he decide to be with me instead of any of them?

CHAPTER TWENTY-ONE

Clare

WHEN I WOKE up, the thoughts of Marco off with some beautiful tanned goddess were still in my head. They'd filled my nightmares the entire night.

Rolling over, I grabbed my phone off the nightstand but saw no missed call and no voicemail. Disappointed, I set it down and sighed. I'd so hoped I would wake up to Marco confessing his love to me and that I'd call him and everything would be fine. I really needed to stop believing that life was going to work out like some fairy-tale from my childhood.

I dragged myself out of bed and opened my curtains to look out into the backyard. Just a few days after the start of fall, the leaves hadn't started to turn, but it would only be a matter of a few weeks before the trees turned red and orange.

For now, it still looked like summer in my yard. The grass was green and the sky was blue with those great big puffy clouds that looked like they'd be nice to sit on.

Summer. I'd always loved that season as my favorite time of year. Now it only reminded me of him.

After another glance at my phone and silently willing him to call, I made my way to the shower to begin my day. Another ordinary day in Hansonville. I didn't hate the thought as much as remember that at one point in time, it wasn't just that for me.

Not ordinary. Not boring. No, this summer had been the best of my life.

For the first time since Colin, I'd taken a chance. I'd somehow pushed away the sadness that had clung to me and the dread of letting someone in that had become part of my very being. For just a few months, I'd been able to shed that oppressive layer that kept me safe yet away from love.

In the spirit of summer's final days, I wore a sundress for what I figured would be one of the last times before the chill of fall settled in. Blue with yellow flowers embroidered on the bottom, it brought out my eyes. I did my hair and makeup, and when I took one last look in the mirror, I had to admit that I felt good.

I looked at my phone every few seconds, but it was no use. He wasn't going to call. I was getting beautiful for no one but me, and it seemed like it was going to be that way forever.

A noise outside that sounded like the backfiring of a truck made me look out the window, and what I saw left me speechless. All spelled out in more red roses than I had ever seen at one time were the words "I love you Clare" and woven into the hundreds of roses were little penguin stuffed animals.

I looked across the lawn and there stood Marco under one of the oak trees. As gorgeous as the first time I saw him at the hospital that first day and as sexy as that night we drove to that bluegrass bar and slow danced, he smiled and waved for me to come out.

I raced down the stairs, nearly falling down the last four or five, and rushed out onto the front porch. The smell of red roses filled the late summer air. Happier than I ever imagined I could be again, I smiled at him and shook my head.

"What is all this?"

"Clare, I'm sorry. I should never have lied to you. I never meant to hurt you. Forgive me or I'm going to have to buy out every florist in this county every day until I convince you to."

As he walked around the message of roses and penguins, I couldn't think of anything but forgiving him. He'd lied, and I'd been stubborn, but now all I wanted was to feel his arms around me again.

When he reached the porch, I stepped toward him and got that hug I'd needed for so long. "I forgive you. Just promise me you'll never lie to me again, though."

"Of course. Never. I promise you that."

He held me close as we looked out over the ocean of flowers on my lawn. I noticed a few people driving by and gawking at us, but for once, I didn't mind being the talk of the town.

"Clare, from the moment I saw you I knew you were special. I knew you were someone I wanted to know. What I didn't know was how much I would fall in love with you."

I turned to smile up at him, but felt Marco shift and before I knew it, he was down on one knee in front of me. Tears welled up in my eyes. Was this really happening? Was I really going to get my happily ever after?

"Marco, I..."

"Clare, I love you. I want you to be the woman I spend the rest of my life with. I want to share everything I have and everything I am with you. I love you. Will you marry me?"

I stared down into his beautiful brown eyes and agreed to be his wife before I ever even looked at the ring he held out. He stood up and took me into his arms, lifting me up and spinning us both around in a circle before placing me down and kissing me.

He slipped the ring on my finger and I looked down at the stunning diamond. "So, future Mrs. Randolph, where would you like to get married?"

I blushed at being called the future Mrs. Randolph, but I loved the sound of it. Looking out at my rose-filled yard, I giggled. "Where it all began. Here."

"At the hospital or the highway?" he teased.

I rolled my eyes and kissed him again. After all the weeks apart, his lips on mine felt as perfect as always.

❖   ❖   ❖

ON A WARM June day with birds chirping in the trees and a gentle breeze, Marco and I, along with the entire town of Hansonville and what seemed like most of Hollywood gathered at my house for the wedding that the tabloids called "The Wedding of The Year."

We didn't think of it as that, though.

For us, it was just two people who found they didn't want to live without one another anymore finally admitting that to themselves. The rest of it—all the glitz and glamour—that meant nothing to us.

I stood inside the house and watched as the guests filed into the backyard. From behind me I heard Emma say, "There she is! I've been looking all over for you!"

"I thought you'd be off looking for Marco's groomsmen," I joked.

Gorgeous in her purple maid of honor dress, she laughed. "That's for during the reception. Right now, my only focus is making sure you're good to go. Are you doing okay with all the reporters and stuff?"

Nodding, I smiled. "I'm good. They've been keeping their distance thanks to the local cops. Who knew they were so interested in helping a local wedding?"

"I saw Marco. He looks so stunning in his tux. I think he might have been a model for them at some point he wears one so well."

Whether he had modeled them or not in the past, I had no idea. None of any of that mattered to me. I fell in love with him when he was a handyman at the Colonial Inn with nothing but a few dollars and no memory.

"So did you two decide where you're going to be living?" she asked with more than a hint of sadness in her eyes.

For months, Marco and I had been working on where we'd finally live after we married. LA seemed to be the natural choice because of his work, and I liked that idea, to be honest. I'd never really felt like I fit in with Hansonville.

But neither of us could bear to leave the place where we fell in love. For all its quirks and small-town ways, it meant too much to both of us.

"We've decided to stay here part of the time, and then live out at the house in LA the rest of the time. To be honest, I'm hoping that time will be during the winter since I wouldn't miss the cold and snow here."

Emma's eyes filled with tears. "I'm so happy to hear that! I'd miss you so much if you went away forever."

Pulling her to me, I hugged her. "Hansonville is where Marco and I found each other. We can't leave now."

From outside, Emma heard her musical cue and hurried toward the back door. Swiveling her head left and right, she said frantically, "It's time! Clare, where's my father? How's he supposed to walk you down the aisle if he isn't here?"

"I'm right here, honey. All ready."

I watched her walk out and down toward the altar, and then I took Emma's father's hand. He'd always been kind to me and since my father had died, he gladly stepped in for him.

I looked at him and smiled as he said, "Your father and I disagreed on a lot of things, Clare, but one thing we always agreed on was how wonderful our two daughters were. I'm sorry he's not here with you today, but he'd be so proud of you."

As I thought of my father, I hoped he would be happy for me.

Jeff walked me down the aisle while I gazed at the man who would become my husband in the next few minutes. Emma was right. He did look incredible in his tux.

Marco smiled when Jeff put my hand in his and whispered to me, "You ready to do this? If you run away now, I can probably hold off the press for a few minutes."

I shook my head at his nervous joking. "I'm not running away anymore."

The minister began to speak, and before long, we said our I do's and heard the words "I now pronounce you man and wife. You may kiss the bride."

Marco kissed me like that first night after the bluegrass bar, and once again, I felt like I was flying. We'd had a long road to travel to get to this place, but I wouldn't have changed a thing.

Well, maybe a few things, but we both got our happily ever after.

"I love you, Clare. Now you're stuck with me."

With a smile, I said, "I love you, Marco. And I can't think of anyone I'd rather be stuck with."

We turned to our guests and walked down the aisle to a chorus of clapping and cheering. My part of the wedding had been fairly small so most of them were famous people I didn't know. It didn't matter. The whole world would see pictures of our wedding soon and that level of exposure was still bizarre to me, but Marco and I were finally together forever and that was the only thing that mattered.

The two of us walked straight into what was now our house and closed the door behind us, desperate for just a few moments of peace before the reception began outside.

"Was I supposed to carry you over the threshold?" Marco asked as he turned to kiss me far more passionately now that we had some privacy.

He was sexiest to me when he was funny. His being in a tux and my husband officially didn't hurt either. He hadn't let go of my hand since we exchanged our vows, and I loved that he didn't.

I shook my head and smiled. "No. I don't think that's necessary. You could do it later once everyone's gone, if you really want to, though."

"Then it's a plan. Once we're alone, you're getting carried across the threshold."

I looked out toward the front porch and remembered that first night. "This is where it all started, you know that?"

"I do. Before I got that truck, I walked out here and just looked at you through the window."

"Isn't that a little stalkerish?"

"In hindsight, yes. But I had to see you."

"Did you?"

"I did. You were in your living room. I only stayed a few minutes. I wanted to talk to you so badly, but I didn't want to be creepy."

"I'm glad you did talk to me. I'm glad you talked to Emma too. Remember our first date?"

"Yep. I was standing outside on your porch holding that penguin hoping I didn't look like a huge idiot."

"You didn't. I still have Petey, you know."

"What I remember most is you dancing that night. You were the most beautiful woman I had ever seen. You always will be."

"What I remember is you climbing up the side of my house and the sex," I said as a blush warmed my cheeks.

He smiled broadly and kissed me again. "Well, I remember that too, but I was trying to be romantic here since it's our wedding day."

"I love you, Marco Randolph."

Pressing his forehead to mine, he said, "And I love you, Clare Randolph."

I took a look around the house that was now the home I shared with Marco before we walked out to the backyard to join everyone for the reception. My whole world had gone from simple and boring to lavish and crazy in a few short months, and I wouldn't have had it any other way.

That night, we'd fly out for our honeymoon in Belize and then our life as a married couple would truly begin. Our story had the happy ending I'd always dreamed of but never truly believed I'd get.

The two of us had made mistakes, but the one thing true had always been the love we shared. We were something special, something big, and that big love we felt required some extra work.

What I knew above all else to be true was that I loved Marco and he loved me. That had never been a lie.

Be sure to read the first standalone book in the Finding The One series, Hard Work, AVAILABLE NOW at all major retailers!

Zane Gilford has lived a blessed life. The only son of the owner of The Gilford House Inn, he's benefitted from his mother's extraordinary success. But Vermont was never where he wanted to be, and the day after graduation, he put the quaint country inn and everything about it behind him and never looked back.

Until now.

The death of his mother left Zane a very wealthy man, but in her will she also left him a surprise. For an entire year, he must run that Vermont inn he's hated all his life if he wants to get one red cent of his inheritance.

Becca Fox has worked her way to the top of the advertising business and has the personal and professional scars to prove it. In her rare time off, she loves visiting her favorite bed and breakfast in the mountains of Vermont. When she finds a new owner running The Gilford House Inn, she wonders if her favorite getaway place has been ruined for her. He's sexy as all hell and incredibly good looking, but he's so cocky and arrogant.

From the first moment he sees her, Zane knows he wants Becca, but to get a woman like her, he's going to have to learn to be a better man than he's ever been. He's got an inn to run and a woman to win. Neither is going to be easy. And time isn't in his favor.

GET YOUR COPY TODAY AT
ALL MAJOR RETAILERS!

ABOUT THE AUTHOR

K.M. Scott writes contemporary romance stories of sexy, intense, and unforgettable love. A New York Times and USA Today bestselling author, she's been in love with romance since reading her first romance novel in junior high (she was a very curious girl!). Under her Gabrielle Bisset name, she writes paranormal and historical romance. She lives in Pennsylvania with a herd of animals and when she's not writing can be found reading or feeding her TV addiction.

Be sure to visit K.M.'s Facebook page for all the latest on her books, along with giveaways and other goodies! And to hear all the news on K.M. Scott books first, sign up for her newsletter today and be sure to visit her website at **www.kmscottbooks.com**

BOOKS BY K.M. SCOTT:

Crash Into Me (Heart of Stone #1)
Fall Into Me (Heart of Stone #2)
Give In To Me (Heart of Stone #3)
Heart of Stone Volume One Box Set
Ever After (Heart of Stone #4)
A Heart of Stone Christmas (Heart of Stone #5)
Return To Me (Heart of Stone #6)
Forever With Me (Heart of Stone #7)
Heart of Stone Volume Two Box Set
Hard As Stone (Heart of Stone #8)
Set In Stone (Heart of Stone #9)
Silent As A Stone (Heart of Stone #10)
Heart of Stone Volume Three Box Set
All of Me (Heart of Stone #11)

Temptation (Club X #1)
Surrender (Club X #2)
Possession (Club X #3)
Satisfaction (Club X #4)
Acceptance (Club X #5)
The Complete Club X Series Box Set

If I Dream (Corrupted Love #1)
If You Fight (Corrupted Love #2)
If We Fall (Corrupted Love #3)
The Corrupted Love Trilogy Box Set

Crave (Addicted To You #1)
Adore (Addicted To You #2)
Shatter (Addicted To You #3)
Claim (Addicted To You #4)
The Addicted To You Box Set

In The Darkness (Project Artemis #1)
After The Storm (Project Artemis #2)

Behind The Scenes (Project Artemis #3)
The Project Artemis Box Set

Hard Work (Finding The One #1)
Big Love (Finding The One #2)

K.M.'S BOOKS ARE IN AUDIOBOOK TOO!

BOOKS BY K.M. SCOTT WRITING AS GABRIELLE BISSET:

Vampire Dreams Revamped (A Sons of Navarus Prequel)
Blood Avenged (Sons of Navarus #1)
Blood Betrayed (Sons of Navarus #2)
Longing (A Sons of Navarus Short Story)
Blood Spirit (Sons of Navarus #3)
The Deepest Cut (A Sons of Navarus Short Story)
Blood Prophecy (Sons of Navarus #4)
Blood Craving (Sons of Navarus #5)
Blood Eclipse (Sons of Navarus #6)
Blood Ascendant (Sons of Navarus #7)
The Sons of Navarus Box Set #1
The Sons of Navarus Box Set #2

Stolen Destiny (Destined Ones Duet #1)
Destiny Redeemed (Destined Ones Duet #2)

Love's Master
Masquerade
The Victorian Erotic Romance Trilogy